Managing Anxiety in School Settings

Managing Anxiety in School Settings dives into the growing topic of anxiety and its implications on students' emotional and academic well-being, providing key insights into how to enable students to be successful inside and outside of the classroom.

This book provides the reader with a tangible set of strategies for all grade levels that can be built into individualized anxiety survival toolkits for students to utilize in a discreet and effective manner both in the classroom and in their daily lives. With real-life examples from Anxious Annie in each chapter, readers build a grounded, fine-grained understanding of anxiety's causes, different varieties, manifestations, social and learning impacts and coping strategies. Breakdowns by grade level take into account which strategies your students will be most open to and best served by.

School counselors and teachers can use this book to work with students individually, in small groups, classes or even entire schools to create anxiety survival toolkits to provide practical strategies that help students combat their anxiety for the rest of their lives.

Anna Duvall is the director of counseling at Lexington High School. In 2015, she was a semifinalist for National School Counselor of the Year.

Crissy Roddy, PhD, is the director of counseling at White Knoll High School. She has presented about anxiety at the state and national levels.

Managing Anxiety in School Settings

Creating a Survival Toolkit
for Students

Anna Duvall and Crissy Roddy

Routledge
Taylor & Francis Group

LONDON AND NEW YORK

First published 2021
by Routledge
52 Vanderbilt Avenue, New York, NY 10017

and by Routledge
2 Park Square, Milton Park, Abingdon, Oxon, OX14 4RN

Routledge is an imprint of the Taylor & Francis Group, an informa business

Library of Congress Cataloging-in-Publication Data
A catalog record for this title has been requested

ISBN: 978-0-367-46226-0 (hbk)
ISBN: 978-0-367-46225-3 (pbk)
ISBN: 978-1-003-02761-4 (ebk)

Typeset in Times New Roman
by MPS Limited, Dehradun

The authors would like to dedicate this book to a number of people who have helped us through this journey:

- Nick, Nicholas, Cayman, Mark, Emerson and Genevieve, you have been a driving force that pushes us to work toward our best. We love you all and could not have completed this labor of love without your support.
- Mary Ka – you are amazing, and we appreciate all of your help.
- Betty Kendrick and Georgia Mason – you have served as mentors and guiding lights for both of us. Because we knew you, we have been changed for good.

We would also like to dedicate this book to all of the students who have allowed us to be a part of their journey toward growth and healthy living.

Table of Contents

Introduction

Anna Duvall and Crissy Roddy are Directors of Counseling at two high schools in Lexington, South Carolina. They've collaborated on many projects and presentations together, addressing topics such as self-care, technology tips and team building for school counselors. As they've worked together, conversations about their students experiencing anxiety kept resurfacing. In doing a little digging, they realized that they were using similar tools to work with their anxious students. They created the Student Anxiety Survival Toolkit and started sharing their ideas at local, state and national conferences.

This book is intended to provide a comprehensive look at student anxiety and how to assist students learning to manage their anxiety. At the beginning of each chapter, Anxious Annie will share some information about her anxiety. Anxious Annie is based on an actual student. Her struggle with anxiety led to the creation of the first Student Anxiety Survival Toolkit. The toolkit worked so well with Annie, the authors wanted to share their ideas with other counselors. This book follows Annie's journey with her anxiety.

1 What is Anxiety?

I'm so nervous all the time. About anything. About everything. I overthink everything. I'm screaming inside but no one on the outside knows it's happening. I feel like I'm just waiting for the next panic attack ... or the next horrible thing to happen. Why do I have to have anxiety? Does anyone else have anxiety besides me? I think other people just get stressed out and I'm the only one who has this horrible anxiety. There is so much pressure on me to do everything right. I can't take the panic attacks ... breaking out into a big sweat in the middle of class and feeling like I'm having a heart attack. I don't know how I'm going to get through this every day.

– Anxious Annie

Introduction

Merriam-Webster's Online Dictionary (https://www.merriam-webster. com/) defines anxiety as an "apprehensive uneasiness or nervousness usually over an impending or anticipated ill: a state of being anxious." It goes on to state that anxiety is also defined by "an abnormal and overwhelming sense of apprehension and fear often marked by physical signs (such as tension, sweating, and increased pulse rate), by doubt concerning the reality and nature of the threat, and by self-doubt about one's capacity to cope with it." While anxiety can be defined using a simple explanation, understanding and treating it is not as simple. Anxiety is very complicated, with various types being diagnosed in different students. It is uniquely defined by different individuals, depending on a number of factors such as age, developmental level, type of anxiety, life experiences and cultural norms.

Some anxiety is a normal emotional and physical reaction to stress (Ginsburg & Kinsman, 2014). The human body responds to threats, and anxiety can help warn an individual to get out of harm's way. Normal anxiety is short-lived and happens only occasionally. It can even be helpful at times, such as providing a student with motivation to get something done. When a stressor presents itself, they may feel anxious until the stressor is removed. For example, a student may feel nervous before a test. The anticipation of the test brings about mild anxiousness. As soon as the test is over the anxiety is removed and the student no longer feels anxious. However, when the test is over and the student continues to excessively worry about their grade, if they will fail the test, if they will fail the subject, if they will fail their grade, they are experiencing anxiety. When anxiety becomes excessive and overwhelms a student to the point that it interferes with daily life activities they may actually have an anxiety disorder (Glasofer, 2019).

Many students who express symptoms of anxiety go on to be diagnosed with anxiety disorders, which is the most common mental health concern for today's youth (Ginsberg & Kinsman, 2014). Although it is the most commonly diagnosed mental health disorder for children, the number of students who have an anxiety disorder is much higher than the number of students diagnosed. The stigma attached to anxiety prevents many students from seeking an accurate diagnosis. Some parents associate anxiety with weakness or as a negative reflection on their parenting practices. They may either refuse to accept that their child has an anxiety disorder, or refuse treatment for the anxiety disorder. Research has not uncovered a direct cause of anxiety. However, some factors have been found to increase the risk of a student developing anxiety over the course of their lifetime: genetics, traumatic life events, parenting styles and abuse. All of these factors may contribute to a predisposition for anxiety.

The Difference between Stress and Anxiety

Stress

For the purposes of this book, stress is defined as a physical, emotional or mental state of tension (Chansky, 2014). Stress is vital for human survival. However, too much stress can be harmful and lead to anxiety. It is not an emotion that begins when a student starts school. Stress can begin while a baby is still in the womb; a mother's stress can be passed on to the fetus. After birth, infants can sense stress from their parents by picking up on their bodily responses to stress (Waters, West, & Berry Mendes, 2014). The child's heart rate increases and they begin to experience the negative emotions the parent is feeling. These reactions to their parent's stress may predispose them to respond negatively to stressors in their own lives as they grow and develop.

Humans experience a broad range of emotions and feelings throughout their lives. Stress is one of those feelings that are a normal part of life. Some common stressors that are experienced by individuals, regardless of location, include emotional problems, divorce, abuse, caring for others, death of a loved one, job loss, chronic illness, moving and relationships. Physical reactions to stress, although dependent on the individual, can include headaches, upset stomach, poor sleep, rapid heartbeat, muscle tension and sweating. Emotional reactions to stress vary as well – fear, anger, depression, irritability, feeling overwhelmed or unmotivated, racing thoughts and worrying. Students at all educational levels will experience various stressors and reactions to events that happen to them. In the school setting, these events could be exams, presentations, procrastination, disorganization, deadlines, working/studying, friendships, peer pressure, social media, relationships, poor sleeping, homework, lack of support, living situations, poverty and abuse. Other stressors may be present as well depending on the student's particular circumstances.

Different life events and occasions will present varying stressors to individuals, some positive and some negative. A student's physical symptoms to both positive and negative stress may present similarly – their heart will start to beat rapidly and they will feel an adrenaline rush through their veins. Whether or not their response is positive or negative to their stress, however, is dependent on the individual's attitude towards the stressor. Scott (2020) reported that positive stress exists when an individual's stress provides them with an opportunity for a positive outcome; there is no threat present. This is unlike negative stress, which an individual perceives as a threat that will lead to a negative outcome. Many students appreciate positive stressors, as they motivate them to complete a task. Completion of that task leads the student to a sense of accomplishment. According to the American Institute of Stress (2019), positive stress can teach a student the power of resilience. Some positive stressors for students include completing a difficult assignment, making a new friend, completing a presentation, winning at a game/competition, productively using their time, trying something new, reaching a goal and getting organized. Overall, positive stress is beneficial and enables students to cope with the stressors they encounter.

Negative stress is the exact opposite of positive stress; students perceive this stress as a threat and react negatively rather than positively to it. MentalHelp.net (2020) characterizes negative stresses as short-term or long-term unpleasant feelings, with the potential to lead to mental and physical problems. Students' self-perception can suffer because negative stress leads them to believe their stress is beyond their coping abilities. Instead of responding with confidence and a positive mindset, students react in fear and start to feel anxious. Some negative stressors include abuse, serious illness or injury, family issues, moving schools, poverty, death of a loved one, divorce, social media, friendships, relationships, sleep issues and academic pressures. When a student states that they are stressed out, they are likely referring to feeling overwhelmed, unhealthy, and exhibiting lower energy and performance levels. Their negative stress may lead them to feel out of their comfort zones and that they are out of control.

Students will experience both positive and negative stress during their schooling. To quote Charles R. Swindoll "Life is 10% what happens to you and 90% how you react to it." Negative stresses can turn into positive stresses if the student manages their emotions appropriately. However, positive stress can turn into negative stress if the student becomes too overwhelmed and perceives a loss of control. Additionally, inappropriately managing negative stress can lead a student to become anxious. Constant negative stress and the inability to deal with it can lead a student to feel chronically unable to manage their emotions. This often leads to anxiety.

Anxiety

All students get stressed from time to time in their lives, but anxiety is not experienced by all students. Some students feel negative stress in response to a particular event, and then it goes away once the event is finished. Many students feel stressed out or briefly anxious about a situation, but this is not anxiety. Students with anxiety are constantly stressed and excessively worried about real and/or imagined circumstances. In addition to feeling overwhelmed with current stressors, students with anxiety are also consumed with perceived future threats.

A student's physical reaction to anxiety is similar to how they react to stress. However, a rapid heartbeat and release of adrenaline are not the only symptoms felt by the anxious student. They may also sweat, experience muscle tension and breathe rapidly. Additionally, their symptoms don't stop once the stressful event is concluded. Their bodies stay in high alert and their anxiety persists even when the threat is gone (Kelly, 2019). For many students with anxiety, their bodies react in a similar fashion to animals in the wild. For example, if a gazelle is happily munching on vegetation but suddenly hears a twig snap behind her, her body goes into high alert. Her heart rate increases, she starts rapidly breathing, her muscles tense and adrenaline pumps through her veins. As she listens for further sounds and looks around, her body goes into fight or flight mode. The gazelle can stay where she is and fight whatever predator (most likely a lion) is getting ready to attack. If she risks staying where she is, she may be attacked by the lion. Although she isn't completely sure whether or not there really is a lion getting ready to attack, she feels like there must be one and is compelled to escape the vegetation and find a safer retreat. As she makes a hasty retreat to higher ground, she turns around to look at her previous location. There is no lion, although she felt certain there must have been one. It was only a bird breaking a branch from a shrub to make a nest. The gazelle is still breathing rapidly and her heart is still pounding. She remains tense for some time after her escape and remains in high alert for the next several hours. Now imagine this situation with a student in a classroom. A number of anxious students have panic attacks, where they experience the same fight or flight response as the gazelle. They feel trapped by a threat, real or imagined, and look for an escape by any means from the classroom.

Anxiety and stress are not interchangeable terms and should not be treated as such. What is stressful to one student may not be stressful to another. What may cause mild stress for one student may cause anxiety in a different student. No one really knows what causes anxiety and no one person has the exact same experience as another. Although stress and anxiety share some of the same physical symptoms, they are not the same emotional experience for students. When a student experiences stress, it is short term. Anxiety is persistent and interferes with a student's ability to live and function normally. With stress, an external trigger is present and it goes away. With anxiety, the trigger may be external but is more often internal and persists whether or not the stressor is present (Anxiety and Depression Association of America, n.d.). Knowing the difference between stress and anxiety and treating the student appropriately is key for school counselors. Anxiety is a serious matter and should not be brushed off as a simple issue of "stressing out" about something. Students with anxiety need others to appreciate that their distress is more intense than a simple passing stressful moment in their lives. These students are battling to manage their anxiety every day and need others to understand how negatively it impacts their lives.

Who Gets Anxiety?

There is no one specific factor that determines whether or not a student will have anxiety (Kelly, 2019). Any student can get anxiety or be diagnosed with an anxiety disorder. However, according to the Anxiety and Depression Association of America (2019) anxiety is more common among girls and women. It may also be more common in children who are abused and/or neglected.

A number of other factors may increase the likelihood of a student having anxiety:

–   Many anxious students have a genetic predisposition towards having anxiety; they are more likely to have anxiety if they have a family member who has it (Felman, 2018).
–   Medical concerns such as an imbalance of chemicals or hormones in the brain may elevate a student's chances of developing anxiety. Additionally, anxiety is often linked with depression or other medical conditions.
–   Environmental factors play a role in a student's development of anxiety. The stressors of childhood, adolescence and puberty can often be too strenuous for a child to manage. This pushes them beyond the realm of normal stress and into anxiety.

- Family environment plays a huge role in shaping a student's socialization skills. A student's ability or inability to function appropriately is often traced back to the family's ability to cope with stressors. Negative and/or anxious child rearing behaviors are linked to higher levels of anxiety in children (Mousavi, Low, & Hashim, 2016).
- Traumatic experiences can often lead students to start experiencing anxiety. Their anxiety may develop due to the trauma they experienced.
- Location matters. Around the world one in four people are diagnosed with anxiety. North Americans experience higher levels of anxiety while East Asians experience the lowest rates of anxiety (Remes, Brayne, van der Linde, & Lafortune, 2016).

Students are faced with new experiences and challenges as they mature. As they learn about the world around them, certain risk factors can elevate their risk of developing anxiety. While a certain amount of anxiety is normal as children develop, some children cannot cope with the stressors of their lives and develop an anxiety disorder.

Symptoms

Students can exhibit a wide variety of behaviors in the classroom. Many negative behaviors exhibited by all students are automatically labeled as misbehavior by teachers and administrators. Therefore, many behaviors related to anxiety are often mistaken for misbehavior in the classroom.

Students at different age and developmental levels may display different symptoms of anxiety. Despite this, many of the examples students give to describe their anxiety are similar:

- I have butterflies in my stomach all of the time.
- I can't even manage starting simple tasks because I'm so overwhelmed.
- I'm trapped inside of my own head and there isn't any escape.
- My heart is pounding so hard I think I'm going to have a heart attack in the middle of class and die.
- I cry a lot because I don't know how to explain what I'm feeling. I don't even understand why it's happening or how to stop it.
- I start to panic even though I know there's nothing to be panicked about. But I can't stop it. I go into a spiral and can't get out.
- I don't want to leave my house – I'm scared I'll never see my mom again if I go to school.
- No one knows I have anxiety. I hide it well, but I'm screaming on the inside.

School counselors are often required to put on their detective hats in order to figure out why a student is misbehaving. If they determine the misbehavior is actually a response to stress, school counselors can then determine if the student is experiencing normal stress or anxiety. Different students present different symptoms in trying to cope with normal stress or their anxiety. While many emotions are similar, an anxious student's developmental level can impact the ways they present their symptoms.

Elementary School

Young students often find it difficult to verbalize exactly what they are feeling. Many speak in general terms, such as happy, sad, angry, or excited. Expressing deeper emotions, such as anxiety, can be difficult for elementary school students. Younger students are at the early stages of growing and learning how to express themselves and they may not be able to convey what exactly is happening to them when they are experiencing anxiety. Additionally, their anxious symptoms can be very similar to other conditions that elementary aged students often experience. Teachers in the elementary school setting often label anxiety as misbehavior in students. For example, what may appear to a teacher as overactive behavior in a student may actually be a symptom of the student's anxiety. Separating symptoms of anxiety from typical elementary school aged behaviors can be confusing for both the student and the teacher. Younger students may truly not understand why they are experiencing anxiety, they just know that they feel worried and/or scared and don't know how to explain it to others.

Students at the elementary school level may exhibit a number of different symptoms. Among them are:

- Excessive and persistent worrying
- Feeling overwhelmed
- Low self-esteem
- Poor sleeping
- Separation anxiety
- Stomach aches
- Headaches
- Specific fears
- Crying
- Fidgeting
- Restlessness
- Irritability
- Tantrums
- Extreme silliness
- Difficulty concentrating and staying focused
- Avoidance and procrastination
- Academic performance decline
- Frequent restroom requests
- Truancy

Middle/Junior High School

Adolescence brings about many changes, both physical and emotional, to middle/junior high school students. While puberty may not have fully erupted for some students, for others it triggers a whirlwind of emotions. The uncertainty of who they are can create stressors for students at this age. They may display a wide range of emotions during the course of a typical day. Unfortunately, many students at this age get into trouble for their misbehavior. For middle/junior high school students with anxiety, some of these misbehaviors might be written off by teachers as typical adolescent behavior and a lack of maturity. Similar to elementary aged students, numerous middle/junior high school students struggle to verbalize what they are feeling. Those with anxiety may experience a greater struggle with verbalizing their anxious symptoms and understanding how to cope with them.

Anxious students in the middle/junior high school setting may exhibit similar symptoms to anxious elementary school students. However, they may also experience additional symptoms; many of these are dependent on their age and developmental level. Their symptoms may include:

- Excessive and persistent worrying
- Feeling overwhelmed
- Overthinking everything
- Low self-esteem
- Muscle tension
- Headaches
- Stomach aches
- Fidgeting
- Restlessness
- Irritability
- Shortness of breath/rapid breathing
- Difficulty concentrating and staying focused
- Avoidance and procrastination
- Academic performance decline
- Frequent restroom requests
- Assuming the worst
- Embarrassment/refusal to speak in front of others
- Truancy

High School

Teenagers are often seen as students experiencing the "roller coaster of emotions" brought on by puberty. They go through emotional ups and downs throughout the day as they work to cope with their changing physical and mental states. As much as all teenagers struggle during their high school years, teens with anxiety encounter deeper levels of conflict within themselves as they attempt to combat their anxious feelings. In addition to trying to continue their journey of self-discovery, high school students with anxiety are often at odds with trying to identify their anxiety and understand why they have it. This struggle can easily continue into adulthood if not addressed.

Symptoms of anxiety may present themselves differently in high school students than in younger students. While younger students may exhibit behaviors that are not easily identifiable as anxiety, many high school students may demonstrate more noticeable symptoms. Some teenagers who are struggling to identify their anxiety may exhibit symptoms that are labeled as misbehavior by teachers.

High school students are at different developmental levels, so their symptoms may appear different from those around them. Teenagers in the earlier stages of puberty may exhibit many of the symptoms that younger students in elementary and middle/junior high school present in the school setting. However, some high school students may be more obvious in describing their symptoms, meaning they may label their symptoms as anxious. Many of the symptoms exhibited by high school students may include:

- Excessive and persistent worrying
- Feeling overwhelmed
- Overthinking everything
- Low self-esteem
- Muscle tension
- Headaches
- Stomach aches
- Poor sleeping
- Fatigue
- Fidgeting
- Restlessness
- Irritability
- Shortness of breath/rapid breathing
- Difficulty concentrating and staying focused
- Academic performance decline
- Frequent restroom requests
- Assuming the worst
- Embarrassment/refusal to speak in front of others
- Avoidance and procrastination
- Potential alcohol/substance abuse
- Suicidal ideation
- Truancy

How/Why Anxiety Has Become a Universal Issue

School counselors report anxiety reaching epidemic levels within the school setting, starting as early as preschool and kindergarten. High academic expectations are being placed on students at very young ages and they are feeling the pressures (McCormac, 2016). Students are feeling anxious and stressed more and more often while not being able to let others around them know what is going on. The need for higher levels of school counselor involvement is becoming clear as they are asked frequently to address student anxiety. Around the world, different school communities promote the high ideals of excellence and academic achievement. There is an increased push to be better, stronger, faster, smarter and more successful than others. This push is affecting students, often negatively in the academic, career and social/emotional realms of their development.

Younger students who don't receive early interventions for their stress often develop anxiety. Many youth develop unhealthy strategies and behaviors for handling their anxiety. If left untreated, these unhealthy strategies continue as they reach adulthood (McCormac, 2016). Many students, especially those in adolescence, lack the capacity to understand and regulate their emotions. They struggle to manage their anxiety, and in many cultures their anxiety is stigmatized. These students will face barriers that may prevent them from getting the help they need in order to treat their anxiety.

The stressors that can lead to anxiety are universal across every continent in the world (Low, 2019). Although some cultures do not use social media, those that do experience the same issues that can create and exacerbate anxiety in students. The pressures on social media to look a certain way, act a certain way, have a certain number of followers and behave in certain ways do not limit themselves to the United States. Bullying and negativity exist on social media around the world. Students no longer have the option of leaving their social and personal issues in the school building at the end of the day. Their issues follow them home on their phones and/or computers and stay with them twenty-four hours a day. Many students don't feel they can unplug and walk away from their phones and/or computers, leading to higher levels of anxiety within youth across the globe.

School counselors and teachers are seeing students with anxiety more often in the classroom (Truluck, 2019). Stressors are the same around the world in schools, with some cultures putting intense pressure on students to academically succeed. These stressors and pressures can take a student's anxiety to increased levels. Additionally, some cultures stigmatize a student who may have mental health issues. This leads to some students having to hide their anxiety from others, which only increases their anxiety.

There is commonality in students of all ages, all ethnic backgrounds and all cultures who experience challenges in feeling anxious (Low, 2019). No matter the location, when a student's basic needs are not being met, their psychological well-being suffers. Ethic minority groups can experience higher levels of risk for anxiety when they are exposed to adverse life events (Washington et al., 2017). Numerous students around the world experience anxiety and lack the coping skills to manage it. In countries that employ them, school counselors are increasingly seeing symptoms of anxiety occurring in students every day.

Conclusion

Anxiety is not always easily defined, nor is it always easily accepted by others. There is no one specific symptom that identifies a student as having anxiety. Culture, age, developmental level and life experiences all play a role in how a student defines their anxiety.

As students learn to understand their anxiety, they can access resources within the school setting. School counselors are perfectly positioned to help students learn more about their anxiety. They can work with students to teach them specific strategies for reducing their anxiety levels and managing their emotions.

It is important students understand what anxiety is and how it differs from everyday stress. Accepting that they are not the only person who has it – that other students around them may also have anxiety – can be a great comfort to them. Discovering why they have anxiety, what they are trying to accomplish in spite of their anxiety and how to decrease their anxiety are all critical components in helping students. In gaining this understanding, students with anxiety can learn how to manage their anxiety for the rest of their lives.

OK. So I get it now that I have anxiety. I'm not a crazy person, even though it feels like it sometimes. And I realize that I'm not the only person that gets anxiety. My school counselor told me there are other students at my school who have anxiety, too, and even some adults have it! I wouldn't wish this on anyone, but I'll admit that it's a little comforting to know other people are going through what I'm going through. Or that they might even understand how I feel when I'm having a panic attack. I know they can't exactly see what I'm going through, but I know they get what's going on inside my mind. It's still going to be really hard to figure all of this out and how I'm going to survive it, but at least I know I'm not alone.

– Anxious Annie

2   How Anxiety Impacts Learning

Every day in school I want to give up. I can't focus on anything in class because I'm so worried I'm going to fail. I constantly worry about how much I might disappoint my parents, my teachers, even myself. I'm worried about the future and how I'm going to be successful when I can't even get through a week at school without having a panic attack. I feel like everyone can see I'm freaking out and I don't want to come back to school. How am I going to pass my classes when I'm so scared all the time? Will I even be able to graduate from high school?

– Anxious Annie

Introduction

Many studies confirm students who report higher levels of anxiety show lower levels of academic achievement and anxiety can negatively affect academic performance (Owens, Stevenson, Hadwin, & Norgate, 2012). In fact, students with a high level of anxiety score lower on IQ and achievement tests than their peers. This could be due to difficulty accessing the attention, analysis, concentration and memory required for academic success and achievement. When a student suffers from anxiety, the majority of their mental capacity is engaged in creating, processing and addressing their anxious thoughts (Ginsburg & Kinsman, 2014). All their attention is focused on alleviating anxiety instead of the lesson presented in the classroom.

Anxious students are more likely to focus their attention on situations they perceive as dangerous or threatening. They are constantly on high alert – worried the worst case scenario will occur. This can be exhausting for the student, which can detract from their learning. It is also interesting to note students of all academic achievement levels can suffer from academic anxiety. Even students who do well on classwork and homework can suffer from test anxiety and do poorly on tests (Bensoussan, 2012).

Review of Recent Statistics and Research

Prevalence of Anxiety

Worry is common among school age children. About 70% of grade school children report they worry "every now and then" (American Academy of Child & Adolescent Psychiatry, n.d.), with the most common worries related to school performance, illness, being teased, making mistakes and physical appearances. The occurrence and severity of childhood worry has steadily increased. In fact, today's high school students are twice as likely to seek mental health services as teens in the 1980s (Twenge, 2015). Everyday worry that most students experience tends to be situation-specific and temporary. This worry is not very intense, usually does not interfere with functioning and the intensity and duration can be controlled. Students can take control of their worry by taking action or problem solving. Anxiety, on the other hand, is longstanding, persistent, and impacts students' cognitive, emotional and physiological well-being.

Anxiety is the most common psychiatric disorder in childhood. Diagnostic interviews conducted by medical professionals with students aged 13–19 indicate 32% had an anxiety disorder, compared with less than 20% with ADHD, 14% with depression and 3% with an eating disorder (Merikangas et al., 2010). The average age of onset for anxiety disorders is six, compared to age 11 with ADHD, and age 15 with substance abuse.

Although anxiety can impact any student at any grade level, specific types of anxiety affect students at different developmental stages. For example, general fears, especially separation anxiety, primarily impact young students, while social anxiety develops later as peer relationships become more important (Merikangas et al., 2010).

Nearly one in three students (31.9%) will meet the criteria for an anxiety disorder diagnosis by the age of 18. And the percentage of students experiencing anxiety is increasing (Child Mind, 2017). Between 2007 and 2012, anxiety disorders in children and teens rose 20% (Data Resource Center for Child & Adolescent Health, 2017). In addition, the rate of hospital admissions for suicidal teenagers has doubled over the past decade (American Academy of Pediatrics, 2017).

Studies have indicated children of low socioeconomic status (SES) experience higher rates of parent-reported mental health problems than children of higher SES. In addition, the lower SES students reported higher rates of unmet mental health needs (Wadsworth & Achenbach, 2005). Students living in poverty experience a unique array of stressors that adversely affect mental health. Low-income communities are often characterized by poor housing, limited resources, inadequate schools, high crime and violence, all of which are associated with adverse mental health outcomes (Leventhal & Brooks-Gunn, 2000; Bradley & Corwyn, 2002; Fowler, Tompsett, Braciszewski, Jacques-Tiura, & Balte, 2009). To complicate this issue, it is estimated that among children experiencing poverty who are in need of mental health care, less than 15% receive services, and even fewer complete treatment (Kataoka, Zhang, & Wells, 2002; Santiago, Kaltman, & Miranda, 2013).

Brain Research and Anxiety

Recent studies have identified parts of the brain that are key factors in the production and processing of anxiety. Using brain imaging technology and neurochemical techniques, scientists determined the amygdala and the hippocampus play significant roles in most anxiety disorders (The Brain from Top to Bottom, n.d.). The amygdala connects the parts of the brain that process incoming signals with the parts of the brain that interpret these signals. Emotional memories are stored in the central part of the amygdala and may play an essential role in anxiety disorders (Henry, 2019). The hippocampus converts events into memories. It is responsible for forming and reconstructing relational memory needed to navigate through complex environments (Columbia University Medical Center, 2018).

In addition to the wear and tear caused by prolonged stress of the amygdala and hippocampus, anxiety has also been shown to impair the development of the prefrontal cortex. The prefrontal cortex is the region of the brain critical for executive functions such as controlling and focusing attention, making, following, and altering plans, controlling impulsive behaviors and developing the ability to hold and incorporate new information in decision making. These executive functioning skills become increasingly important throughout the school years and into adulthood.

Behavioral neuroscience research in animals indicates serious, anxiety-triggering experiences evoke physiological responses that can alter the construction of the developing brain. These experiences cause changes in brain activity and have been shown to have long-term, adverse consequences for learning, behavior and health (National Scientific Council on the Developing Child, 2010). Consequently, anxiety impairs students' ability to learn and to interact socially with others.

Treatment of Anxiety

Early diagnosis and appropriate interventions for students and their families can make a difference in the lives of children with mental disorders (US Department of Health and Human Services, 2000). Treatment for anxiety can involve psychological counseling and therapy, which might include psychotherapy, such as cognitive behavioral therapy (CBT), or a combination of therapy and counseling. Medication can be useful to alleviate the symptoms of anxiety. The antidepressants most widely prescribed for anxiety are SSRIs such as Prozac, Zoloft, Paxil, Lexapro and Celexa.

Data from the 2016 National Survey of Children's Health shows significant treatment gaps for students with anxiety. For example, 80% of students with a diagnosable anxiety disorder are not receiving treatment (Merikangas et al., 2011). Although anxiety is the most common psychiatric disorder in childhood, it has a lower percentage of students receiving treatment (nearly 80% of those with depression receive treatment, compared with 59.3% of those with anxiety issues).

Treatment for anxiety may require long term interventions. The Child/ Adolescent Anxiety Multimodal Extended Long-Term Study followed 319 students who received treatment for pediatric anxiety disorders (Ginsburg et al., 2018). The participants were evaluated each year for four years after treatment. Across all four years, 21.7% of youth were in stable remission, 30% were chronically ill, and 48% relapsed. These findings indicate anxiety disorders in children and adolescents are often chronic and may require longer-term or intermittent treatment beyond acute treatment.

Psychotherapy and medication, along with lifestyle modifications like exercise including yoga, are all effective treatments to alleviate anxiety. However a combination of cognitive behavioral therapy (CBT) and antidepressant medication is the most effective acute or short-term treatment (Bandelow, Michaelis, & Wedekind, 2017).

Educational Impacts

Anxiety has been linked to poor academic performance. In fact, anxiety is a major predictor of impaired academic performance (Child Mind Institute, 2016). Research indicates that students with untreated anxiety disorders are at higher risk to perform poorly in school, miss out on important social experiences and engage in substance abuse (Anxiety and Depression Association of America, n.d.).

Anxiety impacts educational achievement in many of the following ways:

Impact on Working Memory

High levels of academic anxiety can negatively affect working memory (Owens et al., 2012). Working memory is the ability to hold information in the mind for short periods of time (memory) in order to apply it (working). Students with working memory problems have difficulty getting started on tasks in the classroom. This is often because the child's working memory has been overloaded with the amount of instructions received. School tasks that involve intensive working memory are particularly difficult for students affected by anxiety and depression (Owens et al., 2012). Anxious students may be slow to copy things down from the board because they find it hard to remember more than one or two words at a time. They frequently need to check and recheck the original sentence for accuracy. These students have trouble following through on instructions, especially when more than one instruction is given at a time.

The effects of anxiety on working memory can be further explained by Eysenck and Calvo's (2007) processing efficiency theory. This theory states the brain's resources can be drained by its attempt to process increased levels of anxiety leaving few resources available to facilitate learning. Theoretically, the attention demanded by students' anxiety will prevent them from participating in their learning as effectively as someone who is not experiencing anxiety (Kennard, 2018). This effect was shown when Ashcraft and Kirk (2001) studied the performance of students with math anxiety. Their results confirmed that students with high math anxiety demonstrated smaller working memory spans. The reduced working memory capacity led to a pronounced decrease in reaction time and errors when mental addition was performed concurrently with a memory load task.

Results from a study by Owens et al. (2012) show that working memory and academic performance are positively related and anxiety and academic performance are negatively related. Additionally, they found that working memory was a mediator between anxiety and academic performance. These results illustrate how anxiety negatively impacts working memory thereby reducing task performance.

Difficulty Processing Information

To convert new information into long term memory, it must be expanded upon, or connected with, previous learning. If the new information isn't connected, it will not be not be stored properly. Students with excessive anxiety have difficulty connecting new information because their anxiety demands their undivided attention. It interferes with their ability to concentrate (McKibben, 2017).

Even if anxious students have the ability to pay attention in class, their learning is often on a surface level because their cognitive abilities have been overburdened with anxiety (International OCD Foundation, n.d.). These students do not properly connect previously learned information to the new information, which prevents the processing required for storage in long term memory. Because this is an ongoing issue, students often have incomplete knowledge across many different areas of the curriculum. Some experts even believe that severe anxiety is a learning disability because it makes it much more difficult for a student to take in, process, and retrieve information (International OCD Foundation, n.d.).

Other experiments found that anxiety had more effect on how much effort it took to perform a task than on how well the task was actually performed. In other words, anxiety often produced "hidden costs", processing information that was not apparent in performance (Economic and Social Research Council, 2009).

Social Implications in the Classroom

Not only does anxiety impact memory and processing, which makes it hard for students to store and recall information, but it can have negative effects on how students engage in social situations at school. Students with anxiety disorder often display a lack of engagement in the classroom, poor relationships with peers and teachers, and an indifference pursuing interests and planning for the future (Truluck, 2019). Anxious students will avoid or even refuse to participate in activities that make them anxious. This includes obvious triggers like presenting in front of a class, but also things like eating in the cafeteria, changing for gym class and participating in group work. This leads to poor engagement in school and has been identified as a strong predictor of academic failure (Hudley, Daoud, Polanco, Wright-Castro, & Hershberg, 2003).

Anxious students will avoid situations and conditions they fear may cause anxiety. This avoidance may appear to teachers and peers like they are uninterested or underachieving. However, anxious students avoid these situations because they are afraid of making a mistake or being judged. This avoidance, in turn, makes others uncomfortable and results in the student feeling lonely, outcast and isolated.

The difficulties associated with anxiety can cause a student to fall behind across many different areas of the curriculum. This could lead to grade retention, which exacerbates their anxiety about school. Retention has been shown to increase the likelihood that a student will drop out of school. Students who drop out are five times more likely to have been retained than those who graduate (National Center for Education Statistics, 2006). In addition, retention in the early grades can cause disadvantages for children including lower achievement, aggression and dramatically reduced college attendance.

Self-efficacy and self-concept are very important in the study of academic anxiety. Students with high levels of self-efficacy and self-concept tend to have lower levels of academic anxiety. In other words, students who are higher achievers tend to have higher levels of self-efficacy and self-concept. When students do well academically, they tend to feel better about themselves (Dobson, 2012).

Students with anxiety can become easily frustrated resulting in anger, tantrums or meltdowns. An anxious student has an overprotective brain which is quicker to respond to perceived threats. This could happen in response to playground disagreements, unfamiliar situations or people, criticism, disappointment, threat of embarrassment, basically anything that could potentially trigger the feeling that something bad may be about to happen. Therefore, a child who is considered disruptive, oppositional or aggressive may be reacting to unrecognized anxiety.

Absenteeism and Avoidance

Refusing to attend school or the need to escape the learning environment are common issues for anxious students and can have a dramatic impact on their education. Fears of embarrassment, humiliation or failing can result in school absenteeism and avoidance.

Absenteeism and avoidance can occur for several reasons:

– Separation anxiety: Some amount of separation anxiety is normal, but when students don't appropriately adjust to separation, their anxiety makes going to school difficult or even impossible.
– Undiagnosed depression or anxiety: Not knowing why they feel different or sad can cause students to self-isolate, withdraw and avoid school.
– Difficulty sitting still and focusing: The thought of having to sit still and use all their mental capacity to manage their anxious thoughts can be overwhelming.
– Their fight or flight response is always on: The students are on high alert because they are afraid or feel threatened at school.
– Inappropriate coping strategies: Anxious students' avoidance responses could lead to physical attacks on other students or teachers, throwing or pushing things or verbal assaults.
– Performance anxiety: Anxious students may be terrified about the thought of answering questions in class.
– Being trapped in threatening situations: This often leads to frequent trips to the nurse and/or school counselor.
– Realization that school is harder for them than other students, and they are falling behind.
– Fear of not being good enough.
– Being overly self-critical: This can sabotage what they are trying to excel in, like school work.

Although the student has an immediate decline in anxiety when they avoid situations that make them anxious, they are prolonging the effects of their anxiety. Getting behind in school work due to numerous absences often creates a cycle of fear of failure, increased anxiety and avoidance, which leads to more absences.

Conclusion

The negative impact of anxiety on students' academic progress and overall well-being is very clear. Students CANNOT learn when they are highly anxious. Without intervention, these students are at risk for poor school performance, diminished learning capacity and social/emotional problems in school.

Anxiety is prevalent among students of all ages. It is a common issue that all school counselors will encounter. Understanding the physiological implications of anxiety is essential for any mental health professional who works with students. An awareness of how anxiety is treated and how it impacts students in the classroom will lead to better outcomes for students, teachers, parents and school counselors.

Knowing that anxious students may learn and think less efficiently, which significantly affects their learning capability, is key for educational professionals. Also knowing how anxiety manifests itself in absenteeism and school avoidance will assist all adults involved to effectively manage these anxious behaviors.

> *I want to learn and I want to graduate. It's really hard some days, but I want to start having more good days than bad days. I want to get a handle on my anxiety so that I'll actually want to come to school everyday instead of trying to find every reason possible to get picked up early – or just stay home in the first place. I know my parents will love me no matter what and I have to work harder to remember that. It doesn't always feel like it when I feel like I'm ruining my grades, but I have to just keep reminding myself that they do still love me.*
>
> – Anxious Annie

3 Social/Emotional Implications of Anxiety

My emotions are all over the place with my anxiety. A couple of my friends have stopped hanging out with me because they said they couldn't handle all of my 'drama'. My really close friends are more understanding, but even they don't really get what's going on inside my head. It's crushing me and I feel so selfish, like I can't think about anyone or anything but myself. But I'm trapped in my own head and this anxiety is stealing all of the joy out of my life. I'm trying my hardest, but what if that's not good enough? What if no one ever loves me? How am I going to make it as an adult if I can't even handle all of this anxiety right now while I'm young?

– Anxious Annie

Introduction

Anxiety can have a devastating impact on students' social and emotional well-being. For some students, anxiety can trigger inappropriate behavior or exaggerated responses to perceived threats. Excessive anxiety can lead to the avoidance of potential or perceived threats (de Visser et al., 2010; Nesse, 2006). Because students want to avoid negative anxiety symptoms such as panic, phobias and obsessive behaviors, they will actively search for ways to avoid any potential threat. Consequently, students with high levels of anxiety will develop inappropriate avoidant coping strategies (Raffety, Smith, & Ptacek, 1997).

The consequences of avoidance behaviors due to anxiety often have a debilitating effect on students' lives (de Visser et al., 2010; Nesse, 2006). Anxiety makes it harder to try new things, to take risks or to even have the desire to try. Anxious students are constantly trying to avoid the negative feelings of tension, apprehension, and worry associated with anxiety (Beuke, Fischer, & McDowall, 2003), which leads to a low motivation to form social and/or emotional bonds with others.

Students with the most severe forms of anxiety can become completely dominated by their fear, impacting their relationships, emotional regulation and susceptibility to alcohol/substance abuse. These students are at the greatest risk of developing social/emotional difficulties.

Developing and Maintaining Relationships

Anxiety can be detrimental to developing and maintaining relationships. Anxiety limits students' willingness to try new things (Anxiety and Depression Association of America, n.d., Anxiety and Depression) and meet new people. Simple social behaviors like making small talk or eye contact can feel overwhelming to a student with anxiety. For example, anxiety can prevent them from moving out of their comfort zone to introduce themself to a new student. The fear of being judged, embarrassed or humiliated can paralyze anxious students.

Forming social relationships requires vulnerability, the willingness to initiate (and reciprocate) personal interactions and the ability to accept disappointment and hurt. Because relationship outcomes cannot be guaranteed, students experience substantial anxiety maintaining their current relationships as well as pursuing new ones. For some, the perceived fear of failure is too high to risk rejection. This type of anxiety can cause students to avoid school or social interactions altogether, potentially ruining any chance at developing meaningful relationships with new people (Tye, 2015).

The following inappropriate social behaviors are common in anxious students:

Dependence

Some students with anxiety develop an intense desire for closeness to their boyfriend/girlfriend or friends, and become exceedingly dependent on them for support and validation. This overdependence places undue stress on any relationship formed by a student with anxiety. The continual demand for approval will push potential friends away limiting the number of potential friends willing to engage. Additionally, students with anxiety may overvalue their relationships with others, leading to more reliance for validation from their friends or family members (Tye, 2015).

Misplaced Anger

Anxious students may also struggle with anger toward those they feel dependent on, acting out in ways that are destructive to their relationships. For instance, the student may become angry or suspicious in relationships, despite no hard evidence to support their worries. This can lead to accusations, mistrust and doubt. Over time, it can erode the very relationships students are working so hard to maintain.

Over Questioning

Students with anxiety may have trouble with relationships as they struggle with thoughts of abandonment. Anxiety makes it difficult to objectively assess whether a worry is legitimate. Students may be prone to overthinking, indecisiveness, fearing rejection and demanding constant communication. These negative feelings can lead to endless questions or repeated attempts to "understand" what is going on. Their anxiety may rise if a boyfriend/girlfriend or friend does not respond back quickly. The repeated questioning can create feelings of uneasiness or mistrust which leads to all parties feeling frustrated or angry.

Avoidance

At the other end of the spectrum, some students become avoidant of all relationships as a way of dealing with their anxiety. When students experience fear or anxiety they may have the tendency to push others away, shut down, put up emotional walls or self-isolate (Good Therapy, n.d.). This can cause students to close themselves off to protect themselves from potential pain. They may avoid negative emotions by choosing to mask their feelings or not show any vulnerability. Students who are avoidant of close relationships can be viewed as cold, nonassertive, emotionally unavailable, lacking empathy or even stand-offish.

Mental Health Implications

Mental health concerns do not occur randomly, but are a result of a collection of unsuccessful attempts to reduce negative thoughts and emotions, combined with the development of inappropriate avoidant coping strategies. The implementation of counterproductive strategies may initially ease anxiety symptoms, but are ineffective in addressing the long term impact of anxiety. For example, avoiding anxiety by not taking a test might make a student feel better in the short term, but comes with the long-term negative impact on their grades.

Students with anxiety experience emotional responses more intensely than students without anxiety (Borelli, Sbarra, Crowley, & Mayes, 2011). This intense response combined with an increased perception of threat (Pergamin-Hight, Naim, Bakermans-Kranenburg, van IJzendoorn, & Bar-Haim, 2015) can lead to the following issues:

Low Self-Esteem

Students with low self-esteem lack self-confidence. They are self-critical and convinced they are not as good as other students. They fixate on the times they failed rather than when they succeeded. They focus on and tend to exaggerate the negative. For example, they often interpret non critical comments made by friends as an insult or ridicule.

Guindon (2002) asked school counselors to list five characteristics that best describe students with low self-esteem. Over 1000 words were used and the most common are listed below:

Withdrawn/shy/quiet
Insecure
Underachieving
Negative (attitude)
Unhappy
Socially inept
Angry/hostile
Unmotivated
Depressed
Dependent/follower

Students with low self-esteem regularly hide away from social situations and avoid activities they consider challenging. In other words, if social acceptance isn't guaranteed, they may not join in. This may be due to difficulty coping with disappointment when they are not accepted into the friend group. Or their fear of making a mistake, losing, or failing may cause their avoidance. The avoidance of a task or challenge without even trying often signals a fear of failure or a sense of helplessness. They often quit soon after beginning a game or a task, giving up at the first sign of frustration.

The characteristics of students with low self-esteem limit their ability to effectively engage in classroom activities. Students experience mistakes, challenges, failure and learning from those mistakes as a part of their educational journey. Students with low self-esteem will struggle academically if their anxiety is not addressed (Glasofer, 2019a).

Weak Sense of Self-Efficacy

Self-efficacy is defined as self-perception and self-judgment of what we can and cannot do. It is the confidence in the ability to exert control over motivation, behavior and social situations. Students who are low in self-efficacy avoid setting goals, and when they do, have low commitment levels to the goals. They do not have confidence in their abilities to meet any goal. They view difficult tasks as threats to avoid. Anxious students focus on personal failures and negative outcomes, quickly losing confidence in personal abilities. When setbacks happen, they tend to give up quickly. Because they don't have much confidence in their ability to achieve, they are more likely to experience feelings of failure and depression. Stressful situations can be very hard to deal with. And students with low self-efficacy are less resilient (Cherry, 2019) and less likely to bounce back.

Self-efficacy can impact how students perceive situations and how they respond to different situations. Low self-efficacy can lead students to believe tasks are more difficult than they actually are. This can lead to task avoidance, poor time management and increased anxiety. Students' behavior can become erratic and unpredictable when engaging in a task in which they have low self-efficacy.

Self-efficacy determines what goals to pursue, how to go about accomplishing those goals and how to reflect upon performance. Anxious students already avoid challenging situations. The thought of setting a goal may be too overwhelming for them. And the energy required to accomplish a goal may seem impossible to muster.

Separation Anxiety

Separation anxiety is a normal stage of development for infants and toddlers. Young children often experience a period of separation anxiety, but outgrow separation anxiety around three years of age. In some children, separation anxiety can evolve into a more serious condition known as separation anxiety disorder, starting as early as preschool age.

Separation anxiety is the unrealistic worry and excessive fear about separation from home or a primary caregiver (Psychology Today, n.d.). The student fears harm will come to an attachment figure while they are apart. This fear causes extreme anxiety and unwarranted distress which keeps students from participating in normal age appropriate activities. When separation does occur, students seem withdrawn, sad or have difficulty concentrating on work or play.

Separation anxiety can develop after a compelling stressful or traumatic event in a student's life like divorce, moving or the loss of a family member or pet. It can also develop because of the actions taken around the student. Overprotective parenting is one example of how actions taken by caregivers can have a negative impact on children. In fact, separation anxiety may be a manifestation of parental separation anxiety where both parent and child feed off of each other's anxiety. In addition, the fact that children with separation anxiety often have family members with anxiety or other mental health disorders suggests that a vulnerability to the disorder may be inherited.

Specific Phobias

Students diagnosed with a specific phobia demonstrate an excessive and uncontrollable fear of an object or situation that is not normally considered dangerous. The feelings of panic, fear or terror are completely out of proportion to the actual threat. This uncontrollable fear triggers excessive anxiety and disrupts normal age appropriate activities. These students become irrationally afraid when confronted with the particular thing that causes them terror. The trigger for a specific phobia can be almost anything – dogs, flying, blood, the dark, clowns or loud noises. The fear can be triggered directly, by encountering the trigger itself, or indirectly by seeing a picture or hearing others talk about it.

Students with specific phobias will anticipate and avoid the trigger, and this avoidance can greatly interfere with normal activities. Often students are well aware that their fears are exaggerated or irrational, but feel that their anxious reaction is automatic or uncontrollable.

Much is still unknown about the actual cause of specific phobias. Causes may include:

- Negative experiences. Many phobias develop as a result of having a negative experience or panic attack related to a specific object or situation.
- Genetics and environment. There may be a link between specific phobias of a child and the phobia or anxiety of the parents – this could be due to genetics or learned behavior.
- Brain function. Changes in brain functioning also may play a role in developing specific phobias.

Substance Abuse/Health Issues

Substance Abuse

Students with anxiety disorders often search for some kind of relief from their symptoms. And it is not uncommon for people with anxiety disorders to misuse alcohol or drugs (Feldman, 2018a; Truluck, 2019). The National Institute on Drug Abuse estimates individuals with anxiety are twice as likely to suffer from substance abuse as the general population. And two-thirds of teenagers who developed alcohol or substance use disorders had experienced at least one mental health disorder (Conway, Swendsen, Husky, He, & Merikangas, 2016).

These attempts at self-medication usually backfire by intensifying the effects of anxiety. Alcohol and drug use can worsen the psychological and physical symptoms of anxiety, reinforcing the need to use more of these substances in order to function normally (Anxiety and Depression Association of America, n.d.). The result is a cycle of substance abuse that can lead to chemical dependence and addiction.

In addition to forming dependency on illegal drugs and alcohol, students may become dependent on prescription drugs. A common medication prescribed for anxiety is benzodiazepines, which are extremely addictive and can form a dependence in as little as two weeks of regular use.

Health Issues

Physical responses to anxiety involve the immune system, heart and blood vessels and hormone secretion. Hormones help regulate various functions, including brain function and nerve impulses. When the body responds to anxiety, the brain floods the nervous system with hormones and chemicals designed to help respond to a threat. This increases the student's heart rate and breathing rate in order to move more oxygen to the brain. This increase in oxygen to the brain is preparing the body to respond appropriately to an intense situation. With occasional stress, the body returns to normal functioning when the stress passes.

Health issues occur when the fight or flight response is triggered daily by excessive anxiety. Repeated stress and anxiety alerts do not allow the body to return to normal functioning. The constant release of hormones and chemicals designed to respond to a threat are helpful for the occasional high-stress event. However, the long-term exposure to stress hormones can be detrimental to physical health. For example, long-term exposure to cortisol (a stress hormone released by the adrenal glands) can contribute to weight gain. This can weaken the immune system, leaving the body more vulnerable to viral infections and frequent illnesses. These hormones also cause physical reactions such as:

- Difficulty swallowing
- Dizziness
- Dry mouth
- Fast heartbeat
- Chronic fatigue
- Headaches
- Irritability
- Muscle tension
- Nausea
- Nervous energy
- Rapid breathing
- Shortness of breath
- Sweating
- Trembling and twitching

Stress hormones can boost blood sugar levels and triglycerides (blood fats) that are used by the body for fuel. When the excessive fuel in the blood isn't used for physical activities, the chronic anxiety and outpouring of stress hormones can have serious physical consequences, including digestive disorders, muscle tension and soreness, short-term memory loss, premature coronary artery disease and even heart attacks.

All of these physical reactions to anxiety impact the physiological state of an anxious student. Their body's response to the anxiety can be profoundly influenced by their coping style and psychological state. Anxiety doesn't cause illness. Rather, it's the response to anxiety that can cause physical illness.

Conclusion

Students diagnosed with anxiety are at a greater risk of developing other social emotional disorders as well as serious health issues. Anxious students have difficulty developing and maintaining relationships due to their overdependence or avoidance of social interactions. This could be due to their compulsatory attention towards negative feedback and/or information, their reluctance to take risks and try new things or their physical reactions to anxiety. These issues combined with the practice of maladaptive strategies to address their anxious feelings unintentionally maintain their anxiety. Low self-esteem and a weak sense of self efficacy can lead to mental health issues and/or substance abuse.

Anxiety alone does not cause other emotional disorders or illnesses. Rather, it's the responses used to calm anxiety that can have lasting impacts on students' well-being. These responses can be profoundly influenced by students' coping style and psychological state. However, there are things students can do to alter the way they respond to anxiety.

Wow, I can get really overly emotional sometimes when my anxiety is really up there. I want to get a better handle on my anxiety because I want to have better, more positive relationships with people around me. I need to try to explain what's going on with me to my friends when I'm feeling ok, not just when I'm freaking out and having panic attacks. I can't explain it to them the way I want to when I'm all tense and all over the place. I need to talk about it with them when we're just hanging out at lunch. Even if they don't understand, I've got to keep trying to work on my anxiety. I have to work on it for me.

– Anxious Annie

4 Types of Anxiety that Students Experience

"My anxiety gets worse depending on what is causing my stress. Sometimes I'm so scared of being around other people that I get paralyzed with fear and can't speak. Forget about getting up to present in class. I would rather get a failing grade than have to get up in front of everybody and talk. When I have tests in school I start freaking out and have a panic attack. I feel anxious all the time. I have so much anxiety about so many things ... I just don't know what's wrong with me!"

– Anxious Annie

Introduction

Students in today's society have many stressors that create anxiety in their lives. While the majority of these stressors are successfully managed by most students, there are those who cannot manage them. Those same stressors go on to significantly impact some students' ability to function in their daily lives (Way Ahead Mental Health Association, 2016). Excessive worry and anxiety become the norm for these students, which could lead them to being diagnosed with an anxiety disorder (Kelly, 2019).

It is not the role of the school counselor to diagnose a student with a mental disorder. Further, school counselors are not qualified to diagnose students in the school setting. It is imperative, however, for school counselors to know and have a working understanding of what anxiety is and how it affects students. School counselors may find it challenging to identify differences between a student experiencing everyday stress and a student experiencing anxiety. With the advent of the internet, students now have numerous opportunities to research and self-diagnose their symptoms and illnesses. This has led to copious amounts of inaccurate diagnoses of a student's mental health concerns. School counselors are not trained to diagnose a student's symptoms, but are tasked instead with helping the student understand what they are feeling and how to cope with those feelings. Students who are concerned they have anxiety and/or an anxiety disorder should be diagnosed by a medical professional.

School counselors need a working knowledge of the types of anxiety disorders that are officially listed in the most current edition of The Diagnostic and Statistical Manual of Mental Disorders (DSM). The DSM-Fifth Edition (American Psychiatric Association, 2013) provides a great deal of clinical information regarding varying types of anxiety disorders. This manual gives a school counselor the basic knowledge of the criteria for different disorders and how they are diagnosed by a medical professional and/or therapist. Understanding a student's symptoms and potential diagnosis can assist the school counselor in considering how anxiety may be impacting the student's ability to function in the school setting (Anxiety and Depression Association of America, n.d., Treating Anxiety Disorders).

Many students can manage their stress within the school setting. They have learned appropriate strategies to cope with the stressors that manifest themselves during the school day. Some of these stressors are natural occurrences: what will happen on the first day of school, giving a presentation in front of a class, taking a big test, even where to sit at lunch, etc. Many students who encounter these stressors only experience mild to moderate nervousness. Once the experience passes, the student is able to move on with their day and the stressors are forgotten. For a student with anxiety, the stressors do not go away. The student may start worrying about what will happen on the second day of school. Or, not just how they did on the presentation, but if other students thought they were awful and a failure. Or if they failed the test and when the next test will be. Or how many people are staring at them and laughing when they don't know where to sit and have no one to sit with at lunch.

There are almost 300 different mental disorders described in the DSM-5. It would be nearly impossible for a school counselor to know all 300 mental disorders; however, a working knowledge of the major types of anxieties will enable school counselors to understand how to effectively work with them in the school environment with students who are diagnosed with them. Anxiety is among the areas where students experience the greatest struggle in and out of the school setting. Anxiety is an area of concern for students of all ages.

Among the several different types of anxiety disorders, there are specific ones that impact students. These are the anxieties school counselors can focus on to gain better insight into as a means for helping their anxious students. School counselors may observe some students presenting symptoms that fall into the following categories of anxiety disorders: Generalized Anxiety Disorder, Social Anxiety Disorder, Posttraumatic Stress Disorder, Obsessive–Compulsive Disorder and Panic Disorder (Rauch, 2017).

Generalized Anxiety Disorder

Anxiety is a normal part of living and is an emotional reaction to stress (Low, 2019). However, it is important to distinguish between the normal anxieties experienced by most students and those experienced by students with Generalized Anxiety Disorder. For instance, a student may have a long and stressful day at school which leads to tiredness and achy muscles at the end of that day. Meanwhile, a student with Generalized Anxiety Disorder may experience the same stressful day but with a physically longer lasting impact. Their tiredness becomes a constant fatigue that does not end when the stressors end. They may become restless and encounter muscle tension that lasts for months.

Students who are diagnosed with Generalized Anxiety Disorder suffer from excessive amounts of worry and anxiety. They are not just worried about a specific stressor, but are also worried and anxious about any number of events happening in their lives. Their worry feels over-whelming and difficult to control; minor difficulties they experience compound into excessive worry (Anxiety and Depression Association of America, n.d., General Anxiety Disorder). While they may not appear to have any worries, students with Generalized Anxiety Disorder are con-stantly seeking approval from others around them. They also worry about and strive for perfection and may be very hard on themselves when perfection is not reached. Their worry is unrelenting and goes on day after day.

A student with Generalized Anxiety Disorder may present their symp-toms at home in a variety of ways. Their symptoms may manifest physi-cally as well as emotionally (Glasofer, 2019b). At home, parents may observe their child exhibiting an inability to sleep or displaying higher levels of restlessness than other children their age. On the contrary, the child may also experience fatigue and irritability. They may experience health problems or start to have interpersonal problems with family members. Always expecting the worst case scenario becomes the norm for these students. Their bodies feel the effects through physical symptoms such as headaches, muscle tension and gastrointestinal issues. Daily living is negatively impacted in the home and the student does not experience the same level of life enjoyment as their surrounding family members (Glasofer, 2019a).

Symptoms of Generalized Anxiety are not limited to home. In the school setting, students may experience numerous difficulties. Their grades may begin to suffer due to their anxiety. In order to avoid anxiety provoking situations, they may be late to school and/or class. Punctuality becomes less important than avoiding stressors that increase anxiety for students.

Peer relationships may also suffer for students with Generalized Anxiety Disorder. Friendships may become strained due to a lack of understanding between the anxious student and others. It may be difficult for an anxious student's friend to understand why they are avoiding certain situations or being irritable toward them. Generalized Anxiety Disorder can negatively affect areas for which a student normally feels enthusiastic – sports, clubs and other extracurricular activities.

Generalized Anxiety Disorder may cause some students to shift their excessive worry from the rational to the irrational. They may begin to fear natural disasters, in spite of a lack of evidence that one will happen. For example, a child with Generalized Anxiety Disorder may have lived through a rainstorm that lasted for several days and flooded the creek behind their home. Now, every time it rains heavily the child is convinced that the creek will flood. Further, they worry that the creek will rise so much it will carry the house away. They are convinced that it will flood every time it rains. This irrational worry leads the child to question what the weather will be each morning, which in turn leads the child to worry unreasonably that the weather may change during the school day. They may become more fixated on impending rainstorms than their schoolwork and their grades begin to suffer.

While it is considered normal anxiety when a student worries about an upcoming test, a student with Generalized Anxiety Disorder may worry constantly both before and after the test. Taking the test doesn't end their worry – the anxiety becomes chronic and disrupts different areas of their lives. It interferes with their schoolwork, their relationships with others and their interactions with their family. When this goes on for months without any respite, the student may be diagnosed by a physician or therapist with Generalized Anxiety Disorder.

Social Anxiety Disorder

Butterflies in a student's stomach can be a natural feeling before standing up in front of the entire class to give a presentation. This situation is not an everyday occurrence and can be intimidating for a student. Other social situations, such as starting at a new school and walking into a classroom for the first time, can also bring about sweaty palms and a rapid heartbeat. Everyday life presents stressors that all students must manage as they engage in different social situations. The butterflies, sweaty palms and rapid heart rate are normal reactions to stress. However, when a student faces a nonthreatening social interaction and has these extreme reactions to the stress caused by the social interaction, they may be diagnosed as having a Social Anxiety Disorder.

Social Anxiety Disorder goes beyond a student being shy or feeling a little self-conscious. A student diagnosed with this type of disorder may experience overwhelming anxiety and disproportionate levels of self-consciousness during everyday situations (Anxiety and Depression Association of America, n.d., Social Anxiety Disorder). They live in daily fear that everyone around them is scrutinizing their every move and negatively judging what they say. Social Anxiety Disorder extends specifically to social interactions. Even non-threatening social situations are overwhelming and disabling to a student, their anxiety and fear outweigh any actual threat presented in the situation. The scrutiny of others impairs their ability to engage in social interactions.

Many of the symptoms of Social Anxiety Disorder are readily visible to others. A teacher may notice visible signs when these students are forced to interact with their peers. The student may exhibit extreme discomfort and hesitate to engage with others. For example, a middle school teacher divides his class into groups to work on a project. Within the group of students, he notices that the student with Social Anxiety Disorder is reluctant to make eye contact with other group members. The student mumbles when asked to contribute to the conversation and behaves in a passive manner as the group interacts. The student doesn't join the group conversation to discuss the project and stays on the fringe of conversation. On the day of the group presentation, the student is absent from school. The entire time the group works together, the student with Social Anxiety Disorder is intensely fearful of being viewed negatively by their peers. It is safer for the student to disengage and get a lower grade than to risk engaging with others in the group.

Less visible signs and symptoms of Social Anxiety Disorder are harder to observe. They may be masked by other symptoms, leading an adult to wrongly assume the student is just shy or socially awkward. The student may present themselves to others as quiet or easily tongue-tied in conversation. On the inside, the student is very fearful of being embarrassed or humiliated by others if they talk. They may not eat at school and appear to others as if they are not hungry; they are afraid of what others will think of what they eat, how they eat it, how much they eat, how they chew, etc. Some students may even engage in alcohol or drug use as a means for enabling them to function in social interactions with others. Other students with Social Anxiety Disorder actively engage in avoidance techniques in order to stay away from having to interact with others in social situations. They sit alone, refuse to initiate conversations with others and do not accept invitations to spend time with other students. Some students with Social Anxiety Disorder begin to experience anticipatory anxiety when they come to know realize they will have to engage in social situations.

While some social activities can be successfully avoided by a student with Social Anxiety Disorder, the quality of their life is extremely diminished by their disorder. The student misses out on a number of opportunities to gain self-confidence and experience positive interactions with other students. Their overwhelming anxiety significantly impairs their ability to engage in everyday activities without enduring intense fear. They feel powerless to stop the disruption to their daily lives.

Posttraumatic Stress Disorder

Posttraumatic Stress Disorder is not as common as other anxiety disorders as it is a condition that occurs in individuals who have experienced or witnessed a very serious life threatening event or trauma. During the course of their lives, students may experience or witness any number of stressful or traumatic events. Over time the stress and anxiety from the event fades and life moves on. Instead of the anxiety of the event relinquishing over time, a student diagnosed with Posttraumatic Stress Disorder experiences severe anxiety and distress that can continue for months or even years (Anxiety and Depression Association of America, n.d., Posttraumatic Stress Disprder). This disorder can be debilitating to a student as they try to navigate their daily lives while also feeling stuck in fight-or-flight mode in order to protect themselves.

Not every student who encounters or witnesses a traumatic event will be diagnosed with Posttraumatic Stress Disorder. Most students will understandably show fear, apprehension, or sadness after a traumatic event. As time goes on, they recover and move on with their lives. Some students may be more at risk for developing Posttraumatic Stress Disorder due to being directly involved in the event, having a lack of support at home and in school, experiencing violence at home, or already having mental health concerns prior to the traumatic event occurring.

Experiencing or witnessing many different traumatic events may lead a student to develop Posttraumatic Stress Disorder, such as the death of a loved one, a serious accident, abuse, a natural disaster, divorce, a physical or sexual assault, a serious illness, violence, or war. The anxiety experienced by the student manifests itself in differing ways and at times may not appear until months or years after the traumatic event has occurred. A student may show different symptoms of Posttraumatic Stress Disorder in the school setting depending on their age, developmental level and type of trauma experienced. Their reactions may change with other stimuli around them in the school. They may exhibit irritability, anger, jumpiness, or trouble concentrating. The student may avoid activities, people or places within the school that remind them of the trauma they experienced.

Flashbacks from the traumatic experience may occur in school, leaving the student feeling retraumatized, as though the event has just reoccurred. Their ways of thinking, learning, understanding and remembering may change. Mood changes and feeling cut off from their peers may also be symptoms for a student with Posttraumatic Stress Disorder. At home, they may experience frequent nightmares and have difficulty sleeping. They may see reminders at home and at school that make it more challenging to move on from the traumatic event. For example, a student may have been the victim of long-term physical abuse in their home. The abuse finally ended when their parent took them and moved out of the abuser's home. In spite of the physical abuse ending, the student begins to withdraw from their peers and becomes jumpy and agitated if their classmates start to get rowdy in the classroom. Students yelling outside at recess cause the student to move away from their peers and stand at the edge of the playground. If a classroom door slams, the student is visibly startled and begins to cry. They are experiencing flashbacks from their physical abuse and are re-experiencing the traumas of that abuse.

A diagnosis of Post-Traumatic Stress Disorder does not define a student's life nor signify they will never be able to get past the trauma. School counselors will benefit from gaining as much information as possible from the family about the traumatic event experienced or witnessed by the student. This will assist the school counselor help the student learn coping skills for their anxieties. If left untreated, these symptoms can create a negative impact on the student's learning and performance in school. A strong support network within the school system will allow the student to rebuild their sense of safety and normalcy instead of feeling trapped and alone within their trauma.

Obsessive-Compulsive Disorder

One of the more easily recognizable anxiety disorders students experience is Obsessive-Compulsive Disorder. This disorder is one of the more readily known anxiety disorders due to its prevalence in today's community. It is seen and discussed on television, the internet, in movies and is even joked about among friends who laugh with each other about their "OCD" tendencies. While many students self diagnose themselves as having Obsessive-Compulsive Disorder, those who are actually diagnosed with it suffer from severe anxiety in their daily lives.

Obsessive-Compulsive Disorder is defined as a person having uncontrollable thoughts or obsessions and behaviors or compulsions that they feel compelled to excessively repeat. To the casual observer, this disorder may not sound as though it is linked with anxiety. On the contrary, Obsessive-Compulsive Disorder is rooted in trying to relieve anxiety by engaging in repetitive thoughts and behaviors (Child Mind Institute, n.d., Teacher's Guide). The individual believes the act of performing repeated routines or rituals will allow them to reduce or eliminate their anxieties and obsessive thoughts (Anxiety and Depression Association of America, n.d., Anxiety Disorders in Children). Many students who are diagnosed with Obsessive-Compulsive Disorder may also be diagnosed with other anxiety disorders as well. Students may start experiencing symptoms at early ages without understanding what is going on. Their obsessions and compulsions may be attributed to being spirited and energetic or very careful and organized.

For a student diagnosed with Obsessive-Compulsive Disorder, their unwanted thoughts can stem from a variety of areas. They may exhibit excessive fears and worries beyond those considered typical of their age. Their obsessive thinking stretches into a worst case scenario mentality and leads them to engage in compulsive behaviors to alleviate their anxiety about their obsessive thoughts. This leads to a cycle of increased anxiety due to intrusive and excessive thoughts and worries, which lead to repeated patterns of behaviors to relieve the anxiety. While the anxiety is temporarily relieved, it begins to build up again and the cycle repeats.

This cycle feels impossible to break for a student with Obsessive-Compulsive Disorder. They see no other relief to the build-up of their anxiety other than to engage in the repeated routines or rituals.

While the obsessions that a student fixates on feel very real to them, they are not founded on any rational basis. Their anxieties stem from worries and fears that may begin as routine concerns, such as losing something, getting sick from germs or staying organized. What differentiates Obsessive-Compulsive Disorder from routine worry and anxiety is its excessiveness and unwantedness. All of the compulsions students engage in with Obsessive-Compulsive Disorder are not realistically connected to the perceived threats the student is experiencing. For example, a young student may be concerned about getting sick. The classroom routine may be for students to wash their hands when they come in from recess to prevent having dirt and germs on their hands when they eat lunch. A student with Obsessive-Compulsive Disorder not only washes their hands when they come in from recess, but also when they get to school in the morning, before and after restroom visits, before and after lunch and other random times in between. If other classmates sneeze or cough in class, the student is compelled to wash their hands. If they touch something they think might be dirty, they are compelled to wash their hands again. They are constantly worried about germs, dirt or being contaminated. If they constantly wash and rewash their hands, they believe they are avoiding exposure to germs and dirt. If they are avoiding exposure to germs and dirt, their anxieties about getting sick are temporarily relieved. This student may be called a "germaphobe" by other students, which may increase the student's anxieties about getting sick. While the student may be conscientious in trying to prevent getting sick, their hand washing rituals will start to interfere with their other school responsibilities and eventually prevent the student from learning. Additionally, their hand washing may begin to extend to other times in the school day leading to more and more time away from instruction.

Many types of obsessive thinking may lead a student to develop an Obsessive-Compulsive Disorder. Some of the more common obsessions seen in students include:

- Showing excessive concern for order and/or symmetry
- Excessively worrying they or a loved one are in danger or will be harmed
- Mentally catastrophizing situations by always assuming the worst case scenario
- Constantly fearing they may lose something valuable
- Engaging in constant "what if" scenarios about the damaging things they could do to themselves or someone else due to their action or inaction
- Obsessively worrying about religious rules or rituals

In order to combat these unwanted and obsessive thoughts, students employ various types of repetitive compulsive behaviors such as counting objects, repeating a behavior until they feel it is exactly right, arranging and rearranging objects very specifically until they feel they are exactly where they must be, checking and rechecking information to make sure nothing has changed, washing their hands, repeating a name, phrase, song or prayer, seeking constant reassurance from others or checking news and weather repeatedly. All of these compulsive behaviors may begin as small habits that reassure the student of their safety. Unfortunately, many times the compulsive behaviors increase in frequency until they begin to impede the student's learning and other activities. Furthermore, if a student is interrupted while engaging in compulsive behaviors, such as counting, they have to start counting all over again. They become stuck on a task until they can get it perfect. This becomes even more time consuming and does not always decrease the student's anxiety as they believe it will.

Panic Disorder

One of the types of anxiety disorders that a school counselor may see more frequently is Panic Disorder. While Generalized Anxiety Disorder is defined by a student's excessive worry, students with Panic Disorder find that their worries and anxieties manifest themselves through physical symptoms. A student with Generalized Anxiety Disorder is constantly in a state of worry; a student with Panic Disorder may experience a panic attack while feeling anxious *or* calm. Panic attacks and Panic Disorders are more difficult to determine in the school setting, as many of the symptoms of a panic attack may be attributed to stress. A student may not have developed the coping skills needed to handle everyday stressors, which leads them to believe they are having a panic attack any time they are stressed.

Panic Disorder may present very differently depending on a student's age and developmental level. Younger students experiencing panic attacks may describe symptoms such as an upset stomach or feeling dizzy and sweaty. Older students' symptoms are more likened to those of a heart attack: shortness of breath, chest pains, tingling and feelings of going crazy. Other medical conditions may include some of these symptoms, so parents need to make certain these symptoms are not attributable to any other medical condition before they seek a diagnosis of Panic Disorder. Additionally, certain medications may produce side effects that mimic those of a panic attack.

Reoccurring panic attacks can be indicative of a Panic Disorder. However, it is important to note having a panic attack does not automatically determine the student has Panic Disorder. Many students will see their school counselor for what they self-diagnose as a panic attack. The delineating factors for a panic attack are different from the regular stressors one may feel during the school day. While a student may feel nervous before a test and call it a panic attack, this does not meet the criteria for a panic attack. Panic attacks are defined by a sudden inundation of intense fear and/or discomfort. This surge of panic may peak within minutes; during which a student may feel at least four of the following symptoms, as defined by the DSM-5 (American Psychiatric Association, 2013):

- Palpitation, pounding heart, or accelerated heart rate
- Sweating
- Trembling or shaking
- Sensations of shortness of breath or smothering
- Feelings of choking
- Chest pain or discomfort
- Nausea or abdominal distress
- Feeling dizzy, unsteady, light-headed, or faint
- Chills or heat sensations
- Paresthesias (numbness or tingling sensations)
- Derealization (feelings of unreality) or depersonalization (being detached from oneself)
- Fear of losing control or "going crazy"
- Fear of dying

When a student who is diagnosed with a Panic Disorder starts having panic attacks, their anxieties can begin to skyrocket. They are fearful of having another panic attack, which increases their anxiety levels and eventually leads to another panic attack. This starts a negative cycle during which a student is in constant fear. School work and learning take a back seat to these fears and anxieties. Because they are afraid of future panic attacks, the student may start to exhibit dysfunctional behaviors in order to avoid triggering additional panic attacks. Avoidance of certain tasks becomes the norm in order to survive their situation and hopefully prevent another panic attack. For example, an elementary aged student may worry about failing math. Therefore, every day in math class the student starts to get anxious and eventually begins having panic attacks at the beginning of math. The student begins to worry about their next panic attack in math, so they begin to worry about math class in their science class. They begin having panic attacks in science class because they are so worried about the impending panic attack they just know they are going to have in math class. Right at the end of science class the student asks to go to the nurse because they have an upset stomach. They stay in the nurse's office through most of the math class and return to class at the end of math. Later in the week, the request to go to the nurse is repeated by the student at the end of science class. Again, the student stays in the nurse's office for most of math class. They believe if they don't go to math class they will stop having panic attacks. Unfortunately, avoidance does not resolve a Panic Disorder or render it cured. Although the student found a short-term solution, it is not a lasting or appropriate solution to the Panic Disorder the student is experiencing.

Conclusion

School counselors are tasked with a myriad of tasks each day in their work. Although diagnosing students with mental disorders is not one of those tasks, it is imperative school counselors and educators be knowledgeable about the types of anxiety disorders that students might be experiencing within the school environment. Whether or not the student has been professionally diagnosed, school counselors must be properly equipped to recognize the differences in the symptoms presented by their students to help them address their anxieties. Despite the fact school counselors are not therapists, their knowledge of different types of anxiety can help students to better understand their anxieties and how to cope with them. Armed with a familiarity in anxiety disorders, school counselors can work with students to assist in providing more positive outcomes in dealing with their anxieties.

> *"While my anxieties make me scared a lot of the time, I'm hoping to learn some ways to be around other people and maybe even talk to them a little. I don't want to feel anxious all the time about everything. I need to get a better grip on what I'm really anxious about instead of thinking I'm anxious about everything. I want to learn some ways to calm down before I have to take a test so that I stop having panic attacks. I know I can figure this out with some help!"*
>
> – Anxious Annie

5 The WHY and WHAT of Anxiety

"I have no idea why I have so much anxiety about everything. I keep getting bogged down by things happening around me and I can't get past them. It's like I'm riding an anxiety bicycle around in circles and I can't stop pedaling. I can't stop the bike and get off. I don't know how to stop my anxiety because I don't even understand why I have it in the first place. I don't know how to make it all stop."

–Anxious Annie

Introduction

The intense symptoms of anxiety combined with feelings of danger, panic and dread can be overwhelming for students. Just the thought of the extreme, uncontrollable responses that are associated with anxiety can paralyze students. It can be preposterous for anxious students to imagine a time when they can control their anxiety because the idea of managing these emotions can be so overwhelming.

Helping students understand why they are experiencing anxiety and why their bodies are reacting in uncontrollable ways will lay the groundwork for their ability to predict, manage and relieve their anxiety.

The WHY

The first step to assist a student to manage their anxiety is to help them understand their "WHY." School counselors can facilitate this step by asking "WHY" questions.

WHY questions are asked for two basic reasons: to learn, know, or understand, or to challenge something. WHY can be a question of curiosity or criticism. Traditionally, school counselors are cautioned not to start questions with the word "why" as it can send off signals of scrutiny and indicate a lack of trust in the student's judgement. WHY questions can also come off as accusatory, condemning and can instantly set off students' defense mechanisms. This is especially true of older children and teenagers who are seeking independence and privacy and want to be treated like adults.

However, the use of the 5 Whys technique can be a powerful tool to help students begin to understand their anxiety. Using the 5 Whys technique can lead students to a deeper understanding of what is actually happening, not just the surface issues, or the student's perception of what is happening. When used as questions of curiosity, "WHY" questions can uncover causal relationships between the cause of, and their reaction to, their anxiety.

Recurring anxiety is often a response to deeper issues. "Quick fixes" may help in the present, but they often solve only the surface issues and do not address the root cause of anxiety. Using the 5 Whys technique can assist students to reveal the underlying causes of their anxiety, so that they can address the real reasons why they are anxious.

Origins of the 5 WHYs Technique

Sakichi Toyoda, a great Japanese inventor, industrialist and the founder of Toyota Industries, developed the 5 Whys technique in the 1930s. Toyoda developed this technique and used it with workers in order to evolve the company's manufacturing processes. If there was a problem on the assembly line, Toyoda would use the 5 WHYs with the line workers to determine where the problem occurred. This allowed workers to problem solve by asking the 5 WHYs until the nature of the problem became clear. Once the root cause of the problem was apparent, the workers found that the solution became clear. It became popular in the 1970s, and Toyota Industries continues to use this technique to solve problems today (Toyota Industries Corporation, n.d.).

The 5 Whys technique can help identify the root cause of a problem. This technique uses a "go and see" philosophy, which means decision making is based on an in-depth understanding of the processes and conditions on the shop floor, rather than reflecting what someone in a boardroom thinks might be happening.

The 5 Whys technique is remarkably simple: when a problem occurs, you drill down to its root cause by asking "WHY?" five times. The goal is to uncover the root cause of the problem, identify a countermeasure and employ it to prevent the issue from recurring.

The discovery of a countermeasure is key. A countermeasure is an action (or technique) that will help the student address their anxiety as it occurs. It is not a solution to the problem, but steps to take to control their response. In this technique, the goal is not to find a solution but to find a way to address the outcomes. Think about that in relation to coping with anxiety. Anxiety will happen. However, it is what the student does to address the anxiety that can impact the outcome of their anxiety.

How to Use the 5 WHYs

Select a Specific Example

As the student describes their anxiety, look for concrete examples of how their anxiety impacts them in the classroom. Examples could be: test anxiety, ability to stay in class, difficulty working in groups, etc. Help the student select one concrete example of how their anxiety is impacting them.

Explain the Process

Explain to the student that they will be asked several questions that start with WHY and their answer will be recorded. It is important to provide the context of the word why: for what reason, purpose, or cause. The student needs to understand these questions are not to assign blame, but to uncover their reason, purpose, or cause.

Asking "WHY?" sounds simple, but answering it requires the student to think seriously about their answer. Don't be surprised if the student says, "This is hard!" The student may need time to compose their thoughts before they can respond. This process engages the student's higher-level thinking skills and requires them to explore reasons, causes and purpose. Answering "WHY" helps the student organize their thoughts to get to the root of their anxiety.

Ask the First "Why?"

Ask why their anxiety is occurring.
    Record their answer.

Ask "Why?" Four More Times

For each of the answers the student generated in Step 3, ask further "WHYs" in succession. Each time, frame the question in response to the answer just received. For example, if the student is scared about sitting alone in the cafeteria, the next why question could be "Why is it important to be with other students when you are at lunch?: or "Why is the cafeteria a scary place when you are sitting by yourself?"

Move quickly from one question to the next – pausing just long enough to record their answers. The goal is to get to the root cause to have the full picture of their anxiety before engaging in discussions or drawing any conclusions.

Know When to Stop

Stop when asking "WHY" produces no more useful responses, and you can go no further. The "5" in 5 WHYs is really just a "rule of thumb."

"WHY?" may be needed a few more times before the root cause of the problem is apparent. In other cases, the root cause may be apparent before the fifth "WHY?" The important point is to stop asking "WHY?" when useful responses are no longer available.

The 5 Whys strategy is a simple and effective tool for uncovering the root of a problem. Younger students may need help converting their thoughts into statements. Older students may need redirection to focus on the "WHY." It can be used in conflict resolution, problem-solving and brainstorming. Further, it works especially well to identify the root of anxiety.

Student Examples of Using the 5 WHYs

Anxious Annie

Annie's background: Annie is an intelligent, happy and outgoing 15 year old. Most of her extended family are educators, many of which hold advanced degrees. She suffers from anxiety, especially test anxiety.

Why do you have test anxiety?
I need to get good grades.

Why are good grades important?
To have happy parents.

Why do you want happy parents?
It makes me feel good when they approve of me.

Why is their approval important?
I want to achieve what my parents achieved.

Why is following in their footsteps important?
I don't want to be the odd man out.

Martin

Martin's background: Martin is a quiet, reserved and timid 16 year old. He lives with his mother and step father. The family dynamics are strained and communication among family members is dominated by the mother.

Why are you having anxiety?
Pressure from my mom to get a job.

Why is it important that you get a job?
Mom wants me to be independent with money.

Why is it important to be independent with money?
To be able to go anywhere without asking for money from mom.

Why do you NOT want to ask for money from mom?
I don't want to be a burden.

Why do you NOT want to be a burden?
I want mom to be proud of me – I want to be enough for her.

Jennings

Jenning's background: Jennings is an intelligent, sensitive and artistic third grade girl. She has issues with occasional anxiety, especially when she gets scared or feels like she doesn't have control of a situation.

Why are you having anxiety?
I am afraid of heights.

Why are you worried about heights?
I have had bad experiences in high places that scared me.

Why did those experiences scare you?
I was afraid of being so high up.

Why is being so high up so scary for you?
I have a better chance of falling.

Why are you afraid of falling?
Because you can fall to your death.

Samuel

Samuel's background: Samuel is an eleventh grade boy who just moved into the school. His parents are divorced and he lives with his mom. Samuel struggles with anxiety complicated by being in a new school setting.

Why do you get anxious when you think about making new friends?
I don't like meeting new people – I like to stick with my old friends.

Why don't you want to meet new people?
If I don't connect with them quickly – I don't want to spend my time on them.

Why don't you want to spend the time it takes to get to know new folks?
I don't need to associate with anyone new. I like the friends I have.

Why don't you want to expand your friend base?
I feel happy with my current friends.

Kiana

Kiana's background: Kiana is a quiet ninth grader who is one of the top students in her grade. She is involved in cheerleading, student council and plays in the school's orchestra program. Kiana suffers from low self-esteem due to her anxiety.

Why are you having anxiety?
I'm failing my class and I'm afraid to ask my teacher for extra help.

Why are you afraid to ask for help?
Because he may think I'm dumb.

Why is what he thinks about you important to you?
Because he's smart, his family is smart, his friends are smart.

Why is the fact he has more education than you stressing you out?
I don't want him to know I'm not smart.

Carmen

Carmen's background: Carmen is a precocious seven year old who is very outspoken. She gets easily upset and worried when she makes any mistakes on her schoolwork. Making a mistake slows her progress and she feels overwhelmed that she's getting behind on her work.

Why are you anxious?
The amount of work I have to do – I don't know how I'll get it all done.

Why are you anxious about getting all of your work done?
Because I want my work to be perfect.

Why do you want your work to be perfect?
I'm like my mom – I try to do everything the best I can

Why is it important for you to do everything to the best of your ability?
That's the way I am – that's the way I was raised.

Ivan

Ivan's background: Ivan is an eighth grader with a shy disposition. His father is in the military and the family has moved several times during his schooling. Ivan has a strong work ethic but struggles with the anxiety of making new friends each time he moves.

Why are you having anxiety?
I don't like starting a new class.

Why is starting a new class scary?
I am worried I will not make friends.

Why is it important to have friends in this new class?
I want to enjoy the class and having friends makes the experience better.

Why is it important that you have a good experience in class?
I'm more engaged, motivated and obligated to do well in a class I have friends in.

Why is it important to be engaged in the class?
If I'm not engaged in the class, I will not have a good work ethic and fail the class.

Miles

Miles' background: Miles is a high school senior who is very excited about going to college next year. Because he got into a physical fight during his junior year, he has struggled with anxiety over continued rumors about him wanting to fight again. Miles has started isolating himself from friends and other students.

Why are you having anxiety?

I don't like people judging me.

Why are you anxious about others making assumptions about you?

I don't want to have a bad reputation.

Why is a good reputation important to you?

I want to be known as a good person.

Why is being known as a good person important?

I want to have a good life.

The WHAT

The second step to help students address their anxiety is to find their WHAT. Understanding the "WHY" helps the student uncover the reasons for their anxiety, but it does not produce change. For change to occur, the focus needs to change from the "WHYs" to the "WHATs" and "HOWs" to determine what is needed and how to change it.

Basic Needs

There are several differing theories addressing the exact number and types of basic psychological needs. Some theories suggest a hierarchy of psychological needs, while others support a combination of different equivalent needs. While all theories of psychological needs offer meaningful insights, for the purpose of this book, basic psychological needs will be categorized into three areas that indicate *what* the student needs:

To Belong

This need is grounded in the innate human need for attachment. The need for attachment plays a central role in the first few years of life, as children are reliant on the help of others for survival. And as children mature into adults, the need grows from not only physical attachments, but attachments by social connections.

To Be in Control

Perhaps the deepest basic need is for a sense of control, independence, power and understanding. This includes the ability to live independently, to understand and influence surroundings and to make decisions.

To Be Valued

This need is for acceptance, support and affection. This need speaks to the human desire to feel significant to, and admired by others. It also demonstrates the need to be perceived as competent, good and respected.

Once the student has learned **WHY** they are experiencing anxiety, the **WHAT** they are seeking is evident.

Student examples:

Anxious Annie: – Annie's last WHY was, "I don't want to be the odd man out." This statement illustrates her need TO BELONG.

Martin:	– Martin' last WHY was, "I want mom to be proud of me – I want to be enough for her." This statement reveals his need TO BE VALUED.
Jennings:	– Jennings' last WHY was, "Because you can fall to your death." This statement reveals Jenning's need to BE IN CONTROL.
Samuel:	– Samuel's last WHY was, "I feel happy with my current friends." This statement reveals his need TO BELONG.
Kiana:	– Kiana's last WHY was, "I don't want him to know I'm not smart." This statement reveals her need TO BE VALUED.
Carmen:	– Carmen's last WHY was, "That's just the way I am – that's the way I was raised." This statement reveals her need TO BE IN CONTROL.
Ivan:	– Ivan's last WHY was, "If I'm not engaged in the class, I will not have a good work ethic and fail the class." This statement reveals his need TO BELONG.
Miles:	– Miles' last WHY was, I want to have a good life." This statement reveals his need TO BE VALUED.

It is imperative for students to connect their why and what to create a deeper understanding of their anxiety. Realization that their anxiety is deeply rooted in an attempt to satisfy a basic need helps them view their anxiety from a different, more educated perspective.

Reason Statement

A Reason Statement is a succinct way to remind students about their Why and What – so they can begin to take control and focus on managing their anxiety. It serves as a reminder that they are not weak, or flawed, but are experiencing a response to satisfy a basic need. Their Reason will help the student face their anxiety with strength and understanding.

A reason statement is a simple sentence highlighting their basic need:
My need _____ (their what) is causing my anxiety.

Student Examples

My need to belong is causing my anxiety – **Anxious Annie**

My need to be valued is causing my anxiety – **Martin**

My need to be in control is causing my anxiety – **Jennings**

My need to belong is causing my anxiety – **Samuel**

My need to be valued is causing my anxiety – **Kiara**

My need to be in control is causing my anxiety – **Carmen**

My need to belong is causing my anxiety – **Ivan**

My need to be valued is causing my anxiety – **Miles**

These Reason Statements shift the student's focus from scary feelings of danger, panic and dread they can't control to the ability to understand their anxiety, which leads to an opportunity to manage it.

Conclusion

When students understand WHY their anxiety is occurring and WHAT basic need they are attempting to satisfy, they possess the insight needed to manage their anxiety. School counselors can assist students to uncover the root cause of their anxiety by using the 5 Whys technique. Students can then determine which basic need they are attempting to meet and create their reason statement.

This simple but powerful process allows the student to view their anxiety from a different perspective. The student now has the ability to objectively analyze the root cause of their anxiety and the behaviors they will use to satisfy their unmet basic need.

"I decided to talk to my school counselor about my anxiety. She told me she's not a therapist but can help me do some figuring out about all of my anxiety. She's going to help me find out why I have so much stress and anxiety. And she said if I start to understand why I have so much anxiety, really dig deep inside of me and figure out why, then I can start to learn what it is I'm trying to do when my anxiety gets in the way. Then I can work on how to handle stuff when it gets tough instead of always having panic attacks. This makes me feel better about my anxiety and maybe I'll start to get better!"

–Anxious Annie

6 The HOW: Using Strategies and Techniques at Different Educational Levels

I wish I could get some kind of control over my anxiety. I get so scared sometimes that I just get paralyzed and certain situations are worse and trigger my anxiety. I can even feel it sometimes when I am going to have a panic attack. I will be sitting in class and feel like my body goes into high alert. I feel like I can't breathe and my mind just starts racing. I wish I could just breathe normally and not feel like I'm getting ready to crawl out of my own skin. I just want to know how to feel good again and not feel like I'm dying.

– Anxious Annie

Now that the student understands their WHY and WHAT, they can discover the HOW in learning to manage their anxiety.

Introduction

Elementary school students do not always have the developmental capabilities to fully understand why they have anxiety. They also may not understand the "WHAT" of their anxiety. Some young students may be able to grasp the general concepts of humans' basic needs: to belong, to be valued and to be in control. While they may not understand the deeper nuances involved in each of these needs, most will at least be able to comprehend what their basic needs are and determine which of these is not being met. By realizing which of their needs is not being met, they may gain a better awareness of the "WHY" for their anxiety.

Young minds are amazing sponges that soak up a great deal of knowledge and ideas in their early stages of learning. Strategies and techniques for combating anxieties can be powerful tools for elementary students to learn. Appropriate strategies are a means for getting control over their anxiety before they develop poor coping mechanisms. Younger students do not always have the self-consciousness of being judged by their peers and therefore readily utilize more strategies and techniques in the classroom. If there is a concern about students feeling singled out, teachers can teach their entire class strategies and techniques for handling their stress and anxiety. Young students, even as young as kindergarteners, can utilize a myriad of strategies for working to manage their anxiety. Being able to use anxiety-reducing strategies and techniques at younger ages enables students to better manage their anxiety and thereby experience better success as they grow older.

Middle/junior high school students as a whole are faced with a number of challenges on any given day. For some, the transition from elementary school to middle/junior high school can trigger high levels of anxiety. Developmentally, many are experiencing puberty and trying their best to navigate the unfamiliar territory of adolescence. This is also an age when students are starting to gain a little more understanding of themselves as individuals while trying to fit in with their peers. Middle/junior high school students feel like they are walking around with a spotlight on them at all times and are sensitive to feeling different. A middle/junior high school student with anxiety can feel hypersensitive about their differences and struggle even more with how to manage their anxiety without standing out or appearing different.

The techniques and strategies used by a middle/junior high school student may be much more discreet than those used by an elementary school student. Even if the technique worked well in elementary school, a middle/junior high school student with anxiety may not use obvious tools for fear of drawing attention to themselves. Overt strategies may be abandoned because of the fear of being singled out and made fun of by their peers. Techniques that require less physical movement or attention are best learned and used by middle/junior high school students.

High school students are still in the throes of puberty and struggling to discover who they are as individuals. Maturity starts to kick in along with a better understanding of their basic needs: to belong, to be in control, and to be valued. The HOW of anxiety makes more sense to them since they are more able to engage in deeper levels of thinking. As they are closer to adulthood than childhood, these students with anxiety start to comprehend just how much it affects their lives. While many understand the why and the what of anxiety, they still grapple with the HOW of their anxiety. With all the other pressures that exist in a teenager's life, the thought of successfully dealing with anxiety can feel overwhelming and impossible.

The strategies and techniques used by high school students with anxiety are still selected by how much discretion can be used by the student to implement them. There may still be a concern about the judgment of other students if their anxiety is discovered, and failure or avoidance may be preferable to some high school students over learning effective strategies to cope with their anxieties. For most high school students, living in the here and now is their daily concern rather than thinking long term. Adding anxiety into the mix makes it even more challenging for a teenager to navigate their daily lives. Many high school students still feel at the mercy of others' opinions of them and feel trapped in the conundrum of using anxiety-reducing techniques or appearing "normal" to their peers.

Anxiety does not stop when a student becomes an adult. Whether going to college, working, or joining the military, an adult with anxiety experiences the real-life WHY and WHAT of their anxiety in more certain terms than a younger person. If they have not learned effective strategies or techniques for handling their anxiety before adulthood, it is not too late to learn strategies to enable them to live with their anxiety. While their anxiety will not stop because they are now adults, they can still successfully learn, work and experience life. In contrast, for some adults anxiety may not begin until sometime in their post-secondary lives. Even though this may be the case for many adults; they can still work to learn and implement strategies to thrive and live rewarding lives. In particular, some adults start to experience anxiety in college, as the college experience brings about entirely new freedoms and responsibilities. Some college students develop anxiety due to their struggle with learning to take on adult responsibilities.

Since anxiety does not stop just because a student graduates high school, adults have to learn strategies and techniques for dealing with their anxiety. Life after high school brings about an entirely new mindset about the "HOW" for coping with anxiety. The desire for others' constant approval can take more of a backseat when determining how to address anxiety. For an adult with anxiety, the strategies and techniques learned at younger ages may make more sense and are familiar and comfortable to use. The ability to see more long-term effects of one's actions can encourage an adult with anxiety to look for additional techniques to better combat their anxiety.

Breathing Techniques

Deep breathing techniques provide students with a simple and effective strategy to address their anxiety. They force a student to take pause and focus on their breath. While shallow breathing only expands the chest cavity, deep breathing forces both the belly and chest cavity to expand. Deep breathing reduces heart rate and demands students to slow down, both mentally and physically. This allows students the ability to remember their WHY and WHAT, and to calm down in the face of overwhelming emotions.

The following exercises can work for different developmental levels. Some are full of imagery to engage active imaginations: thinking about bunnies and snakes, flowers, candles, etc. Others work better for more practical or older students.

All breathing techniques begin with the student sitting comfortably with a tall spine and their shoulders back. Students can either close their eyes or gaze gently down in front of them. Instruct the student to take a few deep breaths to calm their mind and body.

- **Belly Breath:** Place one hand on your belly and the other hand on your chest. Take a deep breath in through the nose for four counts, and then exhale through the nose for four counts, with lips closed. Notice the rise and fall of your chest and belly.
- **Flower Breath:** Imagine you are going to smell a fragrant flower. Take a deep breath in through your nose for four counts, and then exhale through the nose for four counts, with lips closed.

  - This technique adds to the aspect of the students imagining they are smelling a flower.

- **Bunny Breath:** Imagine you are a bunny. Take three quick sniffs through your nose and then do one long exhale through your nose. Wiggle your nose like a bunny!

  - This technique works especially well with hyperactive students. It engages their facial muscles and lets them have fun while addressing their anxiety.

- **Snake Breath:** Inhale slowly through your nose for four counts and breathe out through your mouth with a long, slow hissing sound.

  - This technique works especially well when students have a negative association with their anxiety.

- **Blow Out the Candle:** Imagine you are going to blow out a birthday candle. Take a deep breath in through your nose for four counts, and then slowly exhale through your mouth to blow out the candle.
- **Bee Breath:** Pretend you are a bee! Inhale through your nose, keeping your mouth closed. As you breathe out, make a long "mmm" sound with a closed mouth, pretending to buzz like a bee around the garden. Repeat the bee-humming sound on the next exhale.
- **4-7-8 Breathing:** Breathe in quietly through the nose for 4 seconds, hold the breath for a count of 7 seconds, exhale forcefully through the mouth, pursing the lips and making a "whoosh" sound for 8 seconds.

  - Focusing on the pacing of this breathing technique can shift a student's attention from their anxiety to slowing their breathing and addressing anxiety. The 4-7-8 breathing technique is a breathing pattern developed by Dr. Andrew Weil (Gotter, 2018).

- **Alternate Nostril Breathing:** Close one nostril by placing fingers gently over it. Breathe out, then in, through the uncovered nostril. Switch nostrils.
- **Take 5/Stop Hand Breathing:** Stretch out one hand like a star, or a stop sign. Use the pointer finger of the opposite hand and begin to trace along the hand that is stretched out. Inhale through your nose as you trace up the outside of the thumb, then exhale through your mouth as you trace down along the inside of your thumb. Inhale as they trace up the outside of their pointer finger, exhale as they trace down the inside of their pointer finger...and so on and so forth until all of their fingers have been traced.

Grade-Level Implementation

This strategy is useful for all ages and is one that can be most readily used in any setting. Some students with anxiety may feel very comfortable using these discreet strategies in front of others. Deep breathing may not work for all students; however, it is the most commonly used strategy used to address anxiety.

Elementary School

Deep breathing is an especially useful stress reduction strategy for elementary students. It is easy to use and has proven to increase calmness and decrease stress levels. Using specific breathing strategies that are very visual and descriptive can be attractive to younger students. This enables them to use their imagination and have fun with anxiety reduction. They can also use a visual reminder that goes along with the strategy to better recall what to do and how to use it.

  Some of the deep breathing strategies that work very well for elementary school students with anxiety are Flower Breath, Bunny Breath, Snake Breath, Blow Out the Candle, Bee Breath, 4-7-8 Breathing, and the Take 5/StopHand Breathing. The visualization of some of these strategies, such as Flower Breath, Bunny Breath, Blow Out the Candle and Take 5/Stop Hand Breathing make it easier for younger students to use. These techniques can be taught one on one by the school counselor with the student. School counselors can also teach these anxiety-reducing strategies in small counseling groups or during school counseling classroom lessons. The kinesthetic aspect is very appealing to younger students in elementary school, especially strategies such as the Take 5/Stop Hand Breathing where they are using both of their hands to work through their anxiety. Elementary students with anxiety will also respond well to Belly Breath as they get to place their hands on their belly and actually feel their breathing change as they use the technique. The 4-7-8 Relaxing Breath may be more helpful to older elementary students with anxiety, as they have a better grasp on how the deep breathing strategies are actually helping them to calm down.

Middle/Junior High School

Although students in middle/junior high school can also benefit from deep breathing strategies, they are more reluctant to use any that will draw attention to themselves. Anxiety or not, they do not want the spotlight thrust upon them for any perceived negative reason.

Many deep breathing strategies can be taught one on one by the school counselor where the student can focus solely on their breathing in the quiet environment of the school counselor's office. Intentionally listening to their breathing can help a middle/junior high school student with anxiety to experience the difference in their heart rate and level of calm. Deep breathing strategies that work well for middle/junior high school students with anxiety include Belly Breath, Flower Breath, Blow Out the Candle and 4-7-8 Relaxing Breath. These anxiety-reducing strategies are less noticeable to others and can be used in the classroom setting without drawing any attention to themselves. Unlike some of the deep breathing strategies suited for elementary students that are tactile, these strategies are much more subtle and do not require movement beyond focused breathing. Middle/junior high school students appreciate the discretion of these strategies and are more willing to try these in the classroom when they are feeling anxious.

High School

Many teenagers vacillate between wanting to be noticed by others and wanting to be invisible to their peers. The deep breathing strategies used by a high school student with anxiety will vary depending on their level of maturity and self-consciousness.

High school students with anxiety find deep breathing strategies, such as Belly Breath, 4-7-8 Relaxing Breath and Alternate Nostril Breathing to be constructive in working through their anxiety. School counselors can teach these strategies individually to high school students with anxiety and let them practice them in their office. The high school student can then determine which deep breathing strategies are the most effective in reducing their anxiety and which ones they are most comfortable using. Some high school students may not find deep breathing strategies helpful and may not want to use them at all. Others may want to use the deep breathing strategy, but not in front of other students. School counselors can speak to the student about stepping out of the classroom to get water or to go to the restroom in order to practice deep breathing strategies when needed. School counselors will also want to touch base with the student's teacher so they understand why the student is asking to leave the class.

Post-Secondary

Adults are usually much more willing to use whichever deep breathing strategies they feel are most effective for managing their anxiety. Some adults will have learned deep breathing techniques at younger ages and may still be comfortable using them. Others do not experience anxiety until they become adults and have to learn strategies for the first time.

Depending on the nature of their lifestyles after high school, some adults will use different deep breathing strategies to help with their anxiety. Adults can especially benefit from Belly Breath, 4-7-8 Relaxing Breath and Alternate Nostril Breathing. Most adults have the maturity to understand the benefits of slowing down their heart rate and lowering their blood pressure by practicing deep breathing strategies for their anxiety. Adults will engage in other activities, such as yoga or meditation to help with their anxiety; they may learn deep breathing strategies, such as Deep Belly Breathing or Simple Meditation Breathing through these exercises. In the college classroom, military or work setting, many anxious adults may find it helpful to engage more discreetly in the deep breathing strategies they have learned. Belly Breath and 4-7-8 Relaxing Breath can be useful as a person can engage in these strategies discreetly. Alternate Nostril Breathing can take place more privately in the restroom or when the adult is alone and anxious.

Journaling

Journaling is a technique that empowers students to examine and understand their thought processes associated with anxiety. It can be a starting point to help students create order in their chaos. It allows students the ability to view their situation from a different perspective. It engages both hemispheres of the brain; being both analytical and creative and can assist students in processing difficult events.

Journaling is an opportunity for students to privately express their emotions without fear of what others will think. They do not need to worry about sentence structure, spelling or composition. This "self-expression book" empowers the student to make it what they want it to be and engages the students' creative side.

Journaling can be a powerful tool when used in counseling sessions. One of the best ways to learn about thought processes is to write them down. Counselors can partner with students to examine thoughts and patterns exposed in journals. This can help move student responses from anxious and ruminative to empowered and action-oriented. Additional benefits of journal writing for students include:

- Exploring "big feelings" in a healthy and safe way
- A safe outlet to express emotions that are uncomfortable to share

– Reflecting on thoughts after anxiety has subsided
– Gaining an insight into their motives and the motives of others
– Identifying the positives as well as the negatives
– Exploring and understanding emotions
– Identifying problems, fears and concerns
– Assisting in tracking symptoms to recognize triggers
– Exposing negative thoughts and behaviors

Journaling requires the student to be intentional and prepared. Students can choose to respond to a daily prompt which allows an opportunity to write about a new topic every day. Or, students can choose to keep a feelings journal which may be more beneficial in assisting them in identifying and recognizing emotions in themselves and others. No matter how they choose to journal, they need to:

– Have a pen and paper, or an anxiety survival toolkit, handy at all times
– Write down the thoughts, emotions, and responses experienced when feelings of anxiety are present
– Write every day
– Allow words to flow freely
– Not worry about structure or composition. Be concerned with getting thoughts and feelings written down as they are experiencing them

Examples of journal prompts:

- List the emotions you have RIGHT NOW.
- Write a letter to someone and never send it.
- Do you spend time worrying about what other people think? How does this feel?
- Imagine your anxiety as a monster and write a story about it.
- List all the things that make you happy.
- How do you think other people see you?
- Name three qualities you love about yourself.
- Start with "I remember feeling ..."
- When times get tough, I want to remember _____.
- What does it feel like to try something new?
- List 10 things you are thankful for.
- This week I am looking forward to _____.
- How would you describe yourself to a stranger?
- List your ten best talents.
- What was the best compliment you ever received?
- What is the most unique thing about you? Do you like to hide it or let it show?
- List the things that bring you joy.

- Describe a place where you felt happy.
- What was your greatest fear, and how did you conquer it?
- What is something that you would like to change about yourself? How can you change it?
- Why is it important to have high self esteem?
- How do you know when you've succeeded at something?
- Do positive thoughts promote confidence? How?
- Write about something you have done well recently.
- Write about a time when you made a great choice.
- Write about a time you felt proud of yourself.
- Write about a time when you struggled with something new.

Grade-Level Implementation

Journaling can take different forms depending on the developmental level and needs of the student. One of the strongest attributes of journaling is the lack of judgment associated with it. There is no right or wrong way for anxious students to journal. There are no checks for spelling or grammar, and using complete sentences is not necessary. Journaling may work more effectively for older students and adults; younger students may draw instead of writing words. For some students, it is a matter of getting their anxiety out of their heads by getting it down on paper.

Elementary School

Many young students enjoy the idea of journaling, as it provides a creative outlet for expressing themselves. Elementary school students can take advantage of the positive escape from their anxiety by writing about or drawing out their emotions related to their anxiety. Since they are in the earlier stages of development, they appreciate being able to draw about their anxiety rather than having to write a long paragraph about it. Journaling can also serve as a useful tool for students who may not be as verbally communicative about their anxiety.

Journaling can take many effective forms for elementary students with anxiety – writing, drawing, even photo journaling. If a student enjoys writing, school counselors can provide them with specific prompts to help them engage in positive control of their anxiety. They don't need to write in their journal daily; they may have a list of prompts that help them to gain control over their anxiety at that moment. Letting elementary school students use their imagination in their writing can enable them to see and write a new ending to their anxiety. Likewise, drawing in a journal helps anxious students to visualize their anxiety in a way that allows them to draw what their anxiety feels like so that school counselors and others can better understand their perception of their anxiety. Photo journaling may be helpful for younger students who struggle to put their anxiety into words. They may find that instead of writing or drawing to regain a sense of calm, looking at a collection of photos that are meaningful to them can help to reduce their anxiety levels.

Middle/Junior High School

Students in middle/junior high school may have mixed feelings regarding journaling about their anxiety. Some students may be going through puberty and feel extremely self-conscious about writing about their anxiety or anything having to do with their feelings. Other middle/junior high school students with anxiety will find journaling to be a useful tool because it helps them to feel in more control of their anxiety and understand it more clearly.

As many middle/junior high school students are developmentally in a place of self-centeredness, writing about their anxiety in a journal may be a welcome task. School counselors can share different writing prompts with them or anxious students may choose to write out their feelings in a way that is worthwhile to them. Students with more maturity may benefit from writing out their feelings as they are experiencing anxiety. They can then go back and read about how they were feeling at that moment as a means for identifying more root causes to their anxiety. For those middle/junior high school students who do not enjoy writing, drawing in a journal can assist students in pulling out their anxious feelings in a different way. Their drawings may be effective tools to get to the root of their anxiety. Photo journaling can be an especially effective tool for middle/junior high school students with anxiety; they can look through their photo journals when they feel their anxiety increasing in order to lower it.

High School

Students in the high school setting often have a better grasp on sharing their fears and struggles. Journaling is an excellent strategy to use with high school students with anxiety. Teenagers can journal in order to write down their feelings and thoughts related to their anxiety. Seeing their anxiety written down on paper may provide them with a clarity about the roots of their anxiety that talking about it may not serve. They may even find it works better to identify the causes or notice patterns of behavior regarding their anxiety.

High school students may use writing prompts to assist them in their journal writing. They may not have the exact words to describe their anxiety, so school counselors can provide a topic or specific questions to answer to help them express their emotions. Anxious thoughts and emotions can be written down in any form – words, sentences, poetry, etc. By expressing their anxiety in writing, it enables them to get it out on paper and potentially prevent them from feeling stuck in their negative emotions and anxious feelings. It can feel cathartic to take their anxious feelings that are cycling around in their heads and get them out in the open in the journal. Some high school students who struggle to express their anxiety in words may find that drawing in a journal is a more effective strategy. The student doesn't have to be a skilled artist, which can be a relief to a high schooler. They can draw whatever helps ease their anxiety, even lines across a page. Other students may find that a combination of words and pictures helps release their anxious feelings and thoughts.

Post-Secondary

Journaling is not just an activity for children. Adults can also use journaling as a productive strategy in helping them work through their anxiety. It can bring about a sense of calm as they work to better understand and express their anxiety. Adults who are artistic experience a wide range of benefits from journaling. They appreciate being able to express their range of emotions through a medium that already brings them comfort. College-age students, most of whom are well versed in self-expression due to social media, appreciate journaling as a positive strategy for helping to decrease their anxiety.

Many college students and adults with anxiety can benefit from writing prompts or simple drawing tasks; they don't have to be great or even good writers or artists. These specific strategies allow the adult to focus on their anxiety with more clarity than just randomly writing about many different areas of their lives. However, some adults with anxiety may actually prefer their journaling strategy to include less direction as free expression is a more effective strategy for decreasing their anxiety. Adults who prefer to draw about their anxiety rather than write about it tend to embrace the freedom of expression it gives them without the judgment of their artisticness. At the height of their anxiety, their drawing may be sloppy, but as their anxiety decreases they will observe more focus and accuracy to their drawings. These journal writings and drawings are powerful tools for helping adults organize anxious thoughts and cope with them in appropriate ways.

Positive Self-Talk

Self-talk is the internal narrative, or inner voice, all humans have. Self-talk can be positive or negative, and knowing how it impacts behavior will assist students to make proactive changes to address their anxiety. Sigmund Freud introduced the idea that humans have both conscious and unconscious levels of thought, with unconscious cognitive processes influencing behavior in ways not fully recognized (Cherry, 2019).

Negative self-talk is any thought that limits the ability to make positive changes or the confidence in the ability to do so. Negative self-talk can lead to perceiving events as more stressful than they really are. It may attribute negative motivations to people who are well-meaning and recognize more negatives than positives in situations. In extreme cases, negative self-talk can succumb to rumination, the process of repetitively going over a thought or a problem without solution or completion.

Positive self-talk is the equivalent of having an optimistic voice that always looks on the bright side of any situation. Positive self-talk changes the internal narrative to comments like "I can do better next time" or "I can learn from any mistakes, not be defined by them." It reframes the way students perceive stressful situations with an "I can do this" mindset rather than a negative "This is too hard" one. Positive self-talk leads to self-compassion and an appreciation of what can be accomplished.

One of the most beneficial lessons school counselors can teach students suffering from anxiety is how to alter their negative self-talk. Self-talk greatly affects stress levels in multiple ways and learning how to change negative self-talk to positive self-talk is a key part of effective stress management.

Students usually don't realize how often they engage in negative self-talk, or how much it impacts their behavior. The following strategies can help students become more conscious of their internal dialogue and its content.

- **Journaling:** In addition to journaling about anxiety in general, it can be especially effective for helping students understand the impact of their inner dialogue. School counselors can have the student carry a journal with them to log negative comments as they arise. The student should also log the time, place, and origin of the negative comment. School counselors can partner with students to look for patterns, triggers and ways to change their negative self-talk.
- **Verbal Thought-Stopping:** When the student detects a negative thought, they should say to themself "Stop". A thought-stopping protocol can stop the negative thought mid-stream. Saying "Stop" out loud will be more powerful, and will make the student more aware of how many times they are stopping negative thoughts.
- **Physical Thought-Stopping:** Another negative thought-stopping technique is the rubber-band snap. The student places a rubber band around their wrist. As they notice negative self-talk, they pull the rubber band away from their wrist and let it snap back. This serves as a slightly negative consequence that will make the student more aware of their negative thoughts.

Replace Negative Statements

Once a student is aware of their potentially harmful internal dialogue, they can use the following techniques to reframe their negative thoughts into more positive statements:

- **Milder Wording:** Negative words are usually more powerful than positive words. For example, medical professionals talk about "discomfort" instead of "pain." Since "pain" is a more powerful word, discussing the "pain" level can make the perception of it more intense than discussing the "discomfort" level. Students can use this strategy to address anxiety. Changing the more powerful negative words to neutral ones can help neutralize the experience. Instead of using words like "fear" and "helpless," teach students to use words like "concern" and "unable."

  Some examples of milder wording are:

I am so stupid.	I must be missing something.
This will never work.	I will have to work hard.
I made ANOTHER mistake.	Mistakes help me learn.
This is too hard.	This will take me some time.

- **Change Self-Limiting Statements to Questions:** Self-limiting statements like "I can't do this!" or "This is impossible!" are particularly damaging. They increase anxiety and prevent the student from searching for solutions. Research shows asking questions rather than issuing commands is a more effective way to create change (Scott, 2019). When students' self-talk leads to self-limiting statements, teach them to turn the statement into a question. Asking questions leads to exploration and possibility. This type of self-inquiry accesses the problem-solving areas of the brain allowing students to meet negative thoughts with curiosity instead of fear.

  Some examples of changing limiting statements into questions are:

– I'm not good at this	What am I missing?
– No one ever talks to me.	What can I do to get others to include me?
– This will have to be good enough.	Is this my best work?
– Everyone thinks I'm crazy.	How do other people deal with their anxiety?

Grade-Level Implementation

Students of all levels can benefit from the advantages of using positive self-talk, whether they suffer from anxiety or not. Positive self-talk can remind students of what is positive in their lives and gives them a more optimistic mindset and outlook. Regulating feelings and improving self-confidence are two of the most beneficial aspects of using positive self-talk.

Elementary School

Younger students can work to reduce their anxiety by engaging in positive self-talk. They will most likely need assistance in learning how to reframe their negative thoughts into positive ones, but can work to change their inner monologue to include more positive self-talk.

School counselors can teach elementary students with anxiety to think of things they can say to themselves that are positive rather than negative. When younger students experience anxiety, many are emotionally hard on themselves and believe the internal negative statements about themselves. It takes intentional and consistent work by the student to effectively use positive self-talk as a strategy for handling their anxiety. Visuals and charts work very well for elementary aged students, so a school counselor may create a chart the student can refer to when they are trying to change their negative thinking into positive self-talk. The school counselor can work with the student to determine what positive statements they can say in place of the negative self-talk. Younger students might also find worksheets that list positive self-talk/self-esteem statements to be helpful in better identifying their positive attributes as opposed to their negative ones.

Middle/Junior High School

A great deal of negative self-talk takes place in middle/junior high school settings for most students; the combination of adolescence and puberty provides the unfortunately perfect backdrop for self-doubt and lack of self-esteem. Middle/junior high school students with anxiety face an even greater challenge trying to engage in positive self-talk. This strategy may not be utilized as often by middle/junior high school students due to its difficulty in implementing in the adolescent mind.

Most middle/junior high school students with anxiety who choose to use positive self-talk as a strategy will want to use it discreetly. While this strategy can be easily used internally and is not focused on any external activity, some students may still need a physical reminder, such as a written chart, to help them remember what to say to themselves. School counselors may have to teach the student individually what positive self-talk is and how to use it. Additionally, a school counselor could teach this strategy in a small group setting or as part of a school counseling classroom lesson. Middle/junior high school students may find it easier to complete a check off sheet to help determine when they are engaging in negative rather than positive self-talk. Identifying when their anxiety produces more negativity can assist middle/junior high school students in pinpointing where they can work most productively on reducing their anxiety.

High School

Teenagers are notorious for their struggles with self-esteem. Adding anxiety to those struggles makes it especially challenging for a teenager to navigate through their high school years. Positive self-talk can be particularly effective for high school students with anxiety if they choose to utilize it.

High school students with anxiety may find it difficult to engage in positive self-talk. Most of the time negative self-talk is their first reaction to experiencing anxiety. Teenagers can be very hard on themselves and their anxiety can cause them to be even more unforgiving in anxious situations. Their anxiety causes their inner voice to go straight to negative comments which can decrease their self-esteem. School counselors can work with high school students individually to help them identify when their negative thinking is at its peak. This most often coincides with when they are experiencing their highest levels of anxiety. After identifying when it's happening, school counselors can help high school students engage in positive reframing of their negative thinking. They can work to change their mindsets and from "don't say this" to "say this instead." School counselors can encourage the student to write the positive reframes down if needed. High school students with anxiety can also work with school counselors to identify their strengths. This will allow high school students to pull from those strengths when their anxiety is high and engage in more positive self-talk.

Post-Secondary

Adults with anxiety may find it easier to engage in positive self-talk. This strategy works well for individuals with maturity and a developed sense of self. While negative thinking is certainly a part of their everyday life, adults better comprehend the value of engaging in positive self-talk. The reduction in anxiety and decrease in stress on the body (immune system, cardiovascular) are of great benefit as adults work through their anxiety.

College students may be experiencing adult responsibilities for the first time. Along with this comes a great deal of berating oneself for failing at something they feel they should succeed in. Negative thinking is the knee-jerk reaction for many college students with anxiety. Fortunately, most colleges have counseling centers that can be utilized by students. College counselors can teach college students with anxiety how to change their mindsets from negative to positive by engaging in positive self-talk. Any adult can benefit from positive self-talk, just like any child.

Many working adults with anxiety may find it helpful to have a personally meaningful positive thinking quote posted somewhere in the home and work setting to remind them to use this strategy. It can be framed, or even written on a sticky note, as long as the positive quote is a statement that resonates with the person. Adults with anxiety may also be more attuned to noticing the patterns of their negative thinking. While they better understand their limitations, adults with anxiety also are able to more readily identify their areas for growth. They also have the ability to surround themselves with more positivity and move away from the negative things that are increasing their anxiety.

Cognitive Distractions

Cognitive distraction techniques are used to divert attention away from anxiety and "trick" the brain into concentrating on something else. These cognitive distraction techniques demand focus which takes attention away from the distressing feelings in nearly any situation, and are especially helpful when dealing with anxiety.

Cognitive distraction techniques are designed to "ground" students, or immediately connect students with the present moment. When a student senses their anxiety rising, these techniques can be used discreetly in the classroom, hall, bus or any environment. Students can be taught to proactively switch their focus to activities that will demand attention away from their anxiety.

Some examples of cognitive distraction questions:

−   How many desks are in the room?
−   How many people have brown hair?
−   What is the most popular color of shoes/shirts/backpacks in the room?
−   How many tiles are in the ceiling?
−   What do you smell?
−   How many electrical sockets are in the room?
−   How many animals can you name that start with an "A"?

Examples of cognitive distraction activities:

−   Choose a shape (oval or square) and count everything you can see with that shape.
−   Count by 3s as high as you can.
−   Recite a time table in your head.

Grade-Level Implementation

Cognitive distraction is a creative strategy that allows any age student to put an immediate stop to their anxious thoughts. It serves as a distraction by taking focus off of their anxiety and placing it on a benign topic that temporarily changes their thought pattern. This strategy works well to decrease anxiety at any age as long as the individual is willing to actively engage in the implementation.

Elementary School

Young students can feel overwhelmed by their anxiety, and cognitive distraction strategies can help them regain their balance in an anxious moment. These strategies allow elementary students to calm down by taking their thoughts off their anxiety. Cognitive distraction strategies serve as a stop sign for students when they are caught up in their negative thought spiral. Instead of continually cycling in an unending loop of anxiety, cognitive distraction almost tricks the student into thinking about something else in the here and now before they realize they aren't thinking about their anxiety anymore.

Younger students can be easily distracted from their negative thinking by interjecting cognitive distraction strategies. School counselors can help younger students determine which activity might work best for them, whether it's counting something that is a particular color or the number of a particular item in the room. Elementary school students with anxiety can work individually with their school counselor to try different cognitive distraction strategies in the counselor's office. They may mentally go through a list of animals that start with a specific letter of the alphabet, count the number of colors in the room, or use their five senses to determine what they can see, smell, hear, taste and touch. The student can then practice to determine which strategies work better for them in the classroom when they are experiencing anxiety. It may take some trial and error to determine which cognitive distraction strategies work best for the student; some strategies may work better at different anxious moments for the student. School counselors should inform teachers about cognitive distraction strategies used by students with anxiety so they don't mistake a student's momentary inattention as a behavior problem in the classroom.

Middle/Junior High School

Students with anxiety in middle/junior high school may be more reluctant to engage in any cognitive distraction strategies that require them to look around the classroom and have the possibility of singling them out. Some cognitive distraction strategies only require mental engagement and can be more successful for middle/junior high school students. Cognitively grounding their thoughts without having to move around the classroom will be more attractive to and more effective for middle/junior high school students with anxiety.

While looking around the classroom to count desks or staring at the ceiling to count tiles can feel rather embarrassing to a middle/junior high school student with anxiety, sitting still in their desk and using other cognitive distraction thoughts can be effective. Thinking about all the animals they can name that begin with the letter B, for example, does not require any movement or draw any attention to the student. They can also use their five senses to take in the classroom around them or say the alphabet in their heads backwards and slowly. Some middle/junior high school students with anxiety may be comfortable looking around or moving in order to ground themselves when their anxiety is increasing. School counselors can work individually with anxious students to try out different cognitive distraction strategies in their office before trying them in the classroom. Then the student can determine which of the cognitive distraction strategies is most effective for them in the classroom. Other middle/junior high school students may not be comfortable using cognitive distraction strategies in any fashion.

High School

Teenagers live in the here and now, so cognitive distraction strategies can work well for high school students living with anxiety. Since teens constantly dissect their thoughts, conversations and feelings (both real and perceived), they can easily get caught up in the negative cycles of their anxiety. Cognitive distractions can provide that "stop sign" to derail their anxiety and refocus them on the here and now. Some teenagers with anxiety get "stuck" in their own heads and struggle to mentally move away from their anxiety. These high school students may find success with cognitive distraction strategies.

While teenagers are moving in the direction of becoming more aware of who they are as individuals, many of them are still working through puberty and may not want to draw any attention to themselves. For some high school students with anxiety, cognitive distraction strategies that require physical movement, such as snapping a rubber band on their wrist or standing up and moving around may help reduce anxiety. They may also engage successfully in cognitive distraction strategies, such as using their five senses or saying their alphabet backwards slowly in their heads. If that feels too childish to them, they can choose an object in their line of vision and trace it with their eyes. They can mentally describe it in detail – color, shape, weight, texture, etc., until they feel more distracted from their anxiety. Another cognitive distraction strategy successfully used by high school students is imagining their favorite place and describing it in detail. As with younger students, it will be important for the school counselor to make the classroom teacher aware of the student's use of cognitive distraction strategies to avoid the student getting into trouble.

Post-Secondary

Any adult can find great benefit in using cognitive distraction strategies to deal with daily stressors. Adults with anxiety can lower their anxiety levels by making cognitive distraction strategies part of their daily regime. It is easy to slip into the negative thought cycle and let anxiety steadily increase over minutes, hours, days or weeks. However, utilizing cognitive distraction strategies brings the anxious adult back into the current moment and moves their thought patterns back into focus.

By the time adulthood is reached, many college-aged students have either traveled to or daydreamed about their favorite or dream place/vacation. When anxiety is starting to increase, a mental trip to that happy place can put a stop to the anxious thoughts. This cognitive distraction strategy can be used anytime, anywhere. Other mentally effective cognitive distraction strategies for adults with anxiety may include working out a difficult math problem or playing a memory game. They may also picture an object in their mind and describe it to themselves in great detail. Some adults with anxiety prefer to use physical cognitive distraction strategies, so they may get up and go for a walk to change their surroundings and reduce their anxiety. They may find something that makes them laugh or stand up and engage in a few quick exercises such as jumping jacks or running in place. Additional physical activities such as lighting a candle or taking a shower can provide a welcome distraction to an adult's anxiety.

Mindful Meditation

Mindful meditation can help students cope with anxiety by focusing their awareness on the present situation and focusing clearly and rationally on them. Mindfulness brings awareness to thoughts, sensations and emotions. Mindfulness is about noticing, not trying to stop, the thoughts, sensations and emotions associated with anxiety. Students naturally observe, question, discover and make assumptions. Meditation can teach students how to use this natural process to assist with learning emotional regulation to address anxiety.

Meditation has been proven to improve children's attention-span and focus. A University of California, Los Angeles study (Gregoire, 2013) found second- and third-graders who practiced "mindful" meditation techniques for 30 minutes twice a week for eight weeks had improved behavior and scored higher on tests requiring memory, attention and focus than the non-meditators.

Mindful meditation teaches students to remain aware of what is happening around them and of their feelings in that moment, whether they like it, dislike it or are confused about it. By practicing mindfulness, students increase tolerance for the unpleasant – neither identifying with it nor running from it.

Mindfulness can be viewed as a state of mind, a skill and a practice. There are many mindful meditation exercises, from paying attention to the sounds of ringing bells to visualizing flowers and plants. Here are some mindful meditations students can employ in class:

Posture Pinpoint:

School counselors can have the student close their eyes and focus on their current posture. Call their attention to their breath, to how different parts of their bodies feel and how they are connected to the floor. Then have the student move to a tall, erect posture with their feet flat on the floor and their seat firmly in their chair. Call their attention to their breath, to how different parts of their bodies feel and how their feet connect to the floor. Have the student notice how the two postures feel different.

Mindful Breathing:

Concentrate on your breath.

Your mind will wander.

Notice your mind wandering and return your attention to your breath.

Grade-Level Implementation

Some people may confuse meditation with more alternative viewpoints, making them reluctant to engage in any meditative practices. However, this strategy can help students focus on how they are feeling in the current moment, and allows the student to be more aware of their thoughts and feelings during periods of anxiety. Using meditation as a strategy to reduce anxiety also increases the mindfulness of the student using it.

Elementary School

Elementary students are jumpy like little frogs and love to move around. Being still may present a challenge for them. There are students who will embrace the opportunity to have some stillness and calm in their lives, especially those dealing with anxiety. Younger students with anxiety may lack the focus needed to be more mindful of their thoughts and feelings. Older elementary school students may work with their school counselor to learn meditation strategies that are effective in decreasing their anxiety. Meditation may not be a useful strategy for elementary students who have experienced a serious trauma. This strategy's efficacy will be determined by the student's developmental level and ability to focus their thoughts and energy toward lowering their anxiety levels.

Meditation can be effectively used by both active and passive elementary school students as a strategy to control their anxiety. School counselors can teach young students how to be still and pay attention to their surroundings. Instead of feeling overwhelmed by their anxiety, elementary school students can learn ways to shift their focus to their breathing and how their body reacts to anxiety. Meditation doesn't have to be a strategy that requires students to sit on the floor with legs crossed. Young students may enjoy getting out of their seats and sitting on the floor; this may work more effectively than trying it at their desks. Other students may prefer to meditate in their minds while sitting still in their seats. Elementary school students with anxiety may find better success in a guided meditation, so the school counselor may lead the student through the meditation exercise with verbal cues.

Middle/Junior High School

Meditation can be an effective strategy for this age group to manage their stress levels. Students in the middle/junior high school setting can work to develop their mindfulness in order to relieve their anxiety and increase their engagement in the classroom. They can use meditation to discover ways to relax their bodies, release their negativity and become more aware of their thoughts. Taking a brief moment to pause and refocus their thoughts can reduce their anxiety levels. The breathing techniques used in meditation can have other benefits for decreasing anxiety in students, such as lowering their blood pressure or relaxing their muscles.

When working individually with an anxious adolescent, the school counselor can modify the meditation to meet the needs of the student. Different meditative strategies work differently for students, while some students do not find meditation to be effective at all. Meditation apps can be useful to this age group, as cell phones and social media are almost always available to students. For other anxious students, the school counselor may need to call out specific prompts to lead them through meditative exercises.

Bringing a sense of order to their thoughts will assist students in changing their negative thought patterns and gaining better control over their anxiety. They may also find that meditation works to calm them down if they are in the middle of a panic attack. When anxious students respond to their panic with mindfulness and calm, they can then work with their school counselor to examine where the panic attack came from. This will in turn help the anxious middle/junior high school student to experience more calm when they feel their anxiety starting to increase. Since middle/junior high school students rely a great deal on their peers at this age, it may be easier for a school counselor to teach meditation in a small counseling group or school counseling classroom lesson.

High School

Meditation can be a powerful strategy for anxious high school students. High school students are typically at higher levels of development than middle/junior high school students and are therefore more aware of their thoughts and feelings. Anxious teenagers appreciate how meditation allows them to focus their thoughts on the present moment while disconnecting from their anxiety and negative emotions. They can focus on their breathing and heart rate, and reduce their anxiety. Teenagers who feel overwhelmed by their anxiety often find meditation is an effective strategy to bring calm to their chaos.

School counselors can work with anxious high school students individually to practice different types of meditation to determine what works best for the student. Some high school students may not be comfortable with meditation; other anxiety-reducing strategies may work better. For the student who wants to use meditation, it will be useful for the school counselor to walk the student through different types of meditation. It may not be comfortable for some students to close their eyes, so school counselors can modify how the student uses this strategy both in and outside of the classroom. In the classroom, students may need to use meditation with their eyes open to stay out of trouble with the teacher.

Many high school students with anxiety appreciate the simplicity of concentrating on and counting the sounds they hear for a short period of time. This allows them to refocus their attention on the here and now instead of focusing on their anxiety. It also serves as a tool for lowering the heart rate and increasing their calm. Many meditation strategies work very well for high school students with anxiety – it may take a little trial and error to determine which brings the most relief of the student's anxiety.

Post-Secondary

The daily stressors of adult life can skyrocket anxiety levels. The typical pressures adults are presented with change daily and can increase over time. When anxiety is added to these pressures, many adults struggle to engage in positive and healthy coping strategies. As adulthood can also bring about more health issues, meditation can be helpful in providing the anxious adult with a means to help lower heart rate, blood pressure and aid in learning better breathing techniques. As with other age groups, some adults with anxiety may not find mediation to be helpful for their anxiety. In that case, other strategies may be necessary to use instead.

Meditation strategies can be very effective in reducing anxiety for college students and adults. They can be used anywhere they experience anxiety – the lecture hall, the office, the commute to and from work, in line at the grocery store, paying bills and at home. Depending on the needs of the adult, some meditation strategies work more effectively than others at reducing anxiety. Some adults may be more comfortable closing their eyes to meditate, while others will still want to keep their eyes open. Either way can be effective as long as the individual is committed to the meditation strategy. The end result will be the same, which is to aid the anxious adult in regulating their emotions and becoming more aware of their body's reaction to anxiety. Focusing on the here and now through meditation can help the anxious adult thoroughly examine their negative thoughts. They can then work to change their negative thinking each time they meditate.

Affirmations

An affirmation is a short, simple statement used to bring subconscious thoughts to mind. Research has shown that humans have around 50,000 thoughts a day (No Panic, n.d.). Using affirmations to direct thoughts in a positive direction can be an excellent strategy to alleviate anxiety symptoms. One study (Faubion, 2020) regarding anxiety indicates that people who used positive affirmations during times of stress were 83% more likely to decrease symptoms independently than those who didn't.

Using affirmations has been proven to increase positive thinking in anxious students. Students can memorize affirmations, such as "I am strong," "I am capable," or "I am free of anxiety" to recite to themselves during any anxious situation. When internally reciting affirmations, the student should speak to themselves with a positive, yet firm tone. In addition to internal positive affirmations, students can write affirmations on sticky notes or note cards and place them where they will be seen throughout the day. While those statements may seem simple, they are powerful. The more the student practices positive affirmations, the less room there will be for negative thoughts to creep in.

For a student with anxiety, hearing or seeing a positive affirmation may provide them with a moment of pause when their anxiety levels are high. Using positive affirmations as a strategy for reducing anxiety can provide the calmness that a student needs to effectively lessen their symptoms of anxiety.

There are thousands of affirmations for students to explore. School counselors can have a list for students to reference, or the student can create their own. Here are a few examples:

I breathe in relaxation, I breathe out tension.
I live a calm life.
I am ridding my mind of negative thoughts and filling it
with positive ones.
I am in charge of my mind and body.
I am more and more calm with each deep breath I take.
This too shall pass.
I am attracting positive energy into my body.
I can solve any problems that face me.
I am enough.
I am free of anything that weighs me down.
I have everything I need to be happy.
I have great friends.
I have the ability to overcome my anxiety.
I am safe and in control.
I am strong.
The feelings of panic are leaving my body.
My mind is clearing and I am in control.
I am freeing myself from stress.
I can rid my mind of negative thoughts and fill it with positive ones.
I am now in control.
I am brave.
All is well in my world.
My anxiety does not control me.
I have come so far!
My anxiety may be ugly, but I am beautiful.
I deserve to be happy.
I am proud of everything I have accomplished.
I am unique.
I have lots of energy.
I am peaceful.
I embrace change.
I make friends easily.
I am confident.
I am caring.
I think positive.
I am thankful.
I am courageous.
I am optimistic.
I am beautiful.
I am whole.
I have courage.
I reach my goals.
All is well.
I enjoy learning.

I am very creative.
I am persistent.
I am forgiving.

Grade-Level Implementation

Elementary School

Young students respond well to positive reinforcers in their daily lives, and positive thinking increases their self-esteem and positive outlook. While using positive affirmations can be a powerful tool for reducing anxiety, it does not come naturally to many elementary students. Since this strategy takes a great deal of mental work, using positive affirmations may not work for every young student; other strategies may have to be implemented to reduce their anxiety. For those anxious students who respond well to positive affirmations, they will see an increase in the ability to change and control their negative thinking.

School counselors can work with elementary students to teach them how to use positive affirmations. There are a plethora of positive affirmations available for the anxious student to choose from, so counselors will need to explore various affirmations with the student to determine which ones are meaningful to them. For younger students, the affirmation will work better if it is a short, simple phrase. Longer phrases may be more suitable to older students. The student can choose up to ten different positive affirmations that work best for them and the situations that cause their anxiety.

When the elementary school student is experiencing anxiety, they can repeat the positive affirmations to themselves until they start to feel their anxiety lowering. As their inner voice repeats the affirmations, they are replacing their negative thoughts with positive ones. This strategy enables the student to change their thinking about their anxiety, which in turn helps them better control their emotions caused by their anxiety. Repeatedly using this strategy with anxious elementary school students helps them change their inner dialogue from negative to positive, which, in turn, will decrease their anxiety.

Middle/Junior High School

Adolescence and puberty can bring about a surge of negative thoughts and emotions in middle/junior high school students. These negative thoughts will increase even more for the anxious adolescent student. This is a time when students feel like their every move is being examined under a microscope, and with that scrutiny comes a great deal of self-criticism. The anxious middle/junior high school student gets no relief from the self-criticism, as the negative thought cycle continues and the student struggles to stop it. Positive affirmations can help them to stop this cycle and lower their anxiety.

Positive affirmations can work for many anxious middle/junior high school students. However, not all students will find positive affirmations to be helpful in stopping their negative thoughts. School counselors can work with students to determine which affirmations are most effective in managing their anxiety. The student can choose ten to fifteen affirmations that work best for them, write them down and/or memorize them, and repeat the affirmations when they find their anxiety increasing to interrupt their negative thinking. It won't feel natural for the student to repeat positive affirmations in their heads at first, but over time it will serve to help alleviate the symptoms of their anxiety. Their affirmations will ground them in reality and what they know to be true about themselves, while the negative and irrational thoughts are decreased or stop altogether. Middle/junior high school students can work over time to replace their anxiety with their true and positive selves.

High School

High school students can vacillate between cynical and sincerity within moments, so the use of positive affirmations may have mixed results with them. Anxious teens can be very concerned with how they appear to their peers; affirmations may not have any effect on their self-esteem since peer approval may be more important to them than their own. Anxiety already makes their own negative thoughts difficult to overcome, so if they perceive their peers feel negatively toward them, positive affirmations will not be a useful strategy. School counselors will need to assist the high school student to determine if the use of positive affirmations can be helpful in coping with their anxiety.

For anxious high school students who find positive affirmation to be a useful strategy, the use of an affirmation can remind them of what they are rather than what they are not. This is similar to using positive self-talk, the difference being that positive affirmations are based on positive phrases that describe how the student wants to be. Anxious teenagers can work with their school counselor to determine ten to twenty positive affirmations they can repeat to themselves when feeling anxious. The student can either memorize the affirmations or write them down to consult and repeat when their anxiety increases. There has to be sincere buy-in from the teen in order for this strategy to work. Otherwise, they can repeat the positive affirmation hundreds of times without it working. When this strategy is used successfully, high school students will experience a boost in their confidence and self-esteem. These increases in confidence and self-esteem will then aid in lowering their anxiety.

Post-Secondary

College students and adults in any capacity can benefit from the use of positive affirmations. Since their sense of self is more developed, they are not always dependent on outside sources to determine their inner worth. Adults with anxiety can find a great deal of success using positive affirmations. They may be so accustomed to speaking negatively to themselves that they don't realize the positive effect that positive affirmations can have. Adults with anxiety can start to regain control over their emotions and limit some of the fear that always seems to be present in their daily lives.

Adults can start using this strategy by first observing their thoughts. After pinpointing where their negative thoughts start to create anxiety, they should practice pausing their negative thoughts instead of automatically reacting negatively to them. Pausing their negative thoughts also puts their anxiety on hold which keeps it from increasing. At that moment of pause, positive affirmations can be utilized to replace the negative thoughts. This strategy will have to be repeated each time their anxiety starts to increase; it is not a magic wand that cures an adult of anxiety with one use. After repeated use of positive affirmations, an anxious adult may find they are more effectively managing their anxiety. Adults may have better success than young people with this due to their developmental and maturity levels.

Visualization and Imagery

Visualization and imagery are powerful techniques that use mental images to reduce anxiety. Visualization and imagery involve creating a detailed mental image of a calming and peaceful setting or environment. Similar to daydreaming, these techniques are accomplished through the use of the student's imagination.

Visualization and imagery techniques use cognitive distraction to redirect attention away from stressful situations and toward an alternative focus. These are more intentional strategies used for reducing anxiety in students. They work by using suggestions to the body and unconscious mind to act "as though" the peaceful, safe and beautiful environment were real.

Visualization and imagery can be done most anywhere, as it only requires students' imagination and concentration abilities that are always at their disposal. There is no one correct way to use visualization and/or imagery for anxiety relief. These are a few visualization techniques to use with students:

My Happy Place

– Find a calm space and make yourself comfortable.
– Take a few slow, deep breaths to center your attention and calm your mind.

–   Close your eyes (if you are comfortable doing so).
–   Imagine yourself in a peaceful location like a beach, a mountain, a forest, or a park.
–   Use your five senses to describe your imagined location. What do you. ... See? Smell? Feel? Taste? Hear? Take the time needed to slowly answer each sensory question. Use your answers to paint a picture of the place in your mind. For example, if you are imagining the beach, concentrate on the warmth of the sun on your skin, the smell of the ocean, seaweed and salt spray, and the sound of the waves, wind and seagulls. The more you can involve your senses, the more vivid the entire image will become.
–   Remain within your scene, touring its various sensory aspects for five to ten minutes or until you feel relaxed.

Spidey Sense

Ask students to switch their senses up to a superpower level, just like Spiderman.
    In this moment,

–   What can they hear?
–   What can they see?
–   What can they taste?
–   What can they smell?
–   What can they feel?

    Guide students as they stay in this "Spidey State" for 2–3 minutes.
    This is a great activity for younger students. If the student isn't familiar with Spiderman, this activity can be modified to use any superhero. Selecting a superhero the student identifies with will help this activity come alive for the student. This can be used to help calm a busy mind and bring their awareness to the present moment.

5 to 1

Think of:

5 things you can see	5 things you can touch	5 things you can hear
4 things you can touch	4 things you can hear	4 things you can smell
3 things you can hear	3 things you can smell	3 things you can taste
2 things you can smell	2 things you can taste	2 things you can see
1 thing you can taste	1 thing you can see	1 thing you can touch

Butterfly Bliss

Imagine you're a beautiful butterfly fluttering high in the sky.
    You notice a beautiful garden with lots of colorful flowers beneath you.

You decide you are going to flutter down to explore the garden.

You feel the wind blow against your delicate wings. Imagine that as the wind touches you, it gently blows away any worries, any stress you feel.

As you carefully examine each flower, you feel the sun touch your body and warm you.

Look at the big, puffy clouds floating in the sky. Let them remind you how relaxed and calm you can be whenever you want, just by thinking about it.

Spread your beautiful butterfly wings in a huge stretch.

It feels so good.

Your body is calm and your mind is peaceful.

Beach Bound

Imagine yourself sitting in your favorite spot on a beach.

You see the waves breaking on the beach.

You see the children playing in the sand.

You see the beautiful blue sky with a few puffy white clouds.

You see the seagulls flying, gliding on the beach breeze.

The sun shines brightly and gently warms your skin.

You feel the warmth of the sun melting your muscles into complete relaxation.

You feel the lapping of the warm waves against your toes.

You feel the cool wet sand as you dig in your toes deeply.

You feel the ocean breeze on your face.

You feel the rhythm of the calm waves flow over the sand – it relaxes you.

You hear the waves crashing on the beach.

You hear the children playing.

You hear your favorite music gently playing in the background.

You hear the seagulls calling out to each other.

You smell the sea salt in the air.

You smell suntan lotion.

You smell your fruity drink in your hand.

You pick up some beach sand with your hand.

You feel the course grit of the sand.

The dampness of the sand sticks to your hand.

You rinse off your hand in the warm surf.

Notice how your breathing becomes calm and even.

Inhaling and exhaling slowly and calmly.

Paying attention now, you slow down your breath.

Allow your body to relax, slowly and easily. Release your tension and anxiety, any worries and doubts. Inhaling deeply again – breathe in calm and peacefulness.

Breathe deeply and let the relaxation flow to any part of your body that needs it.

Imagine the beautiful golden warm sun penetrating each and every cell and muscle, making you feel so wonderful and alive!

Grade-Level Implementation

Many students enjoy using these techniques to help alleviate their anxiety because they can be used anywhere without anyone noticing. Everyone daydreams as a means for escaping their current situation. These strategies work well at any age, but more successfully for older students who can imagine positive outcomes to their anxiety.

Elementary School

Visualization and imagery can be powerful strategies for young students in dealing with anxiety. If they learn it at a young age, they can create a better sense of self-awareness and gain better control over their feelings. Since anxiety can start at young ages, elementary school students who have anxiety can learn visualization and imagery and use them as life-long tools. If they are able to master these strategies at a young age, they may experience a decrease in their anxiety as they get older. Many young students naturally have a vivid imagination, so using mental imagery as an anxiety-reducing strategy works easily.

School counselors can teach visualization and imagery individually to students as well as in small counseling groups and entire classrooms of students. Elementary school students with anxiety may best learn to use visualization and imagery one on one in the school counselor's office. The school counselor can work with the student to help them designate their favorite place, whether real or imagined, and use their five senses to describe the place out loud. Creating their favorite place in their mind and describing it out loud to the school counselor will help the student create a rich description of their favorite place. This description is what the student will revisit in their minds when they are experiencing anxiety. Additionally, anxious students may benefit from the school counselor reading a script that guides them through a calming scenario. Small counseling groups and entire classes can close their eyes and participate in this activity as the school counselor reads a guided imagery script. Students will learn to use their imagination to focus on a positive, happy scene instead of their anxiety.

Middle/Junior High School

Middle/junior high school students benefit from learning visualization and imagery strategies to help ease their anxiety. However, students in this age group are in different developmental stages and levels of maturity. Some students who are self-conscious about their anxiety may struggle to use these techniques; they may feel it somehow draws more attention to their problems. Others will be willing to try any strategies to help lower their anxiety. School counselors can work individually with the student to determine if using visualization or imagery will be a helpful strategy. Small counseling groups and school counseling classroom lessons may reach some but not all students as some students in this age group may be too worried about others' reactions to truly engage in the imagery exercise.

Students are not required to close their eyes in order to participate in visualization and imagery to reduce their anxiety. School counselors can clarify this point with middle/junior high school students to encourage them to try these strategies. Anxious students at this age already feel as though they have unnecessary attention being focused on them. This strategy can be taught in the school counselor's office with individual students. They can choose to keep their eyes open or closed.

The essential part of these strategies is the student's ability to internally visualize their favorite place and engage all of their senses. When the student experiences the calming effect that imagery has on their anxiety in the privacy of the school counselor's office, it will help them understand how this strategy can be used in any setting. When the student feels their anxiety increasing in class, they can use imagery to go to their favorite place in their head. No one else in the classroom knows what the student is doing. Using imagery enables the student to focus their thoughts somewhere else instead of staying focused on their anxiety. This strategy can be used as often as needed to help the middle/junior high school student decrease their anxiety.

High School

Students in high school can be just as imaginative as young students. While many are still discovering who they are and may still feel self-conscious about themselves, they are usually more willing to try visualization and imagery as anxiety-reducing strategies. High school students are approaching adulthood and are striving to be in control of their lives, these strategies let them control their thoughts and regain control over their emotions. Going to a calm place in their imagination allows the student to focus on regaining calm feelings. High school students with anxiety can find great success by using visualization and imagery to refocus their positive feelings and lower their anxiety levels.

When working individually with high school students with anxiety, school counselors can guide the student through visualization and imagery with each of their senses. The student can determine their favorite place, describe the place with each of their senses to the school counselor, and create the place in their minds. This activity allows them to fully imagine the place and experience the calming feelings that go along with it. Although many high school students with anxiety are able to navigate visualization and imagery effectively by themselves, some may need to hear a script in order to use this strategy. For high school students who struggle using their imagination, coming up with their own ideas for their favorite place may be challenging. They may not find it easy to create the scenario in their heads without assistance. School counselors can work individually with these students and read a script that describes a calming scenario using the student's senses. This allows the student to better visualize and experience the calming scenario instead of having to create it themselves. When students feel they have a good grasp on a calming scenario in their heads, they can use that scenario in the classroom when they are experiencing anxiety.

Post-Secondary

Adults and college students with anxiety may find visualization and imagery useful in slowing down their minds and allowing them to focus on controlling their thoughts. For those that experience higher levels of anxiety in the lecture hall or work space, having a positive mental escape can lead them to lower anxiety levels. The calming effect of visualization and imagery works to help adults put a stop to their negative thought cycles and decrease their anxious feelings. College students and adults with anxiety also appreciate the positive and healthy side effects of using visualization and imagery. It can help lower blood pressure, heart rate, and enhance sleeping patterns.

For adults, the effectiveness of visualization and imagery as anxiety-reducing strategies depends on the willingness of the person to truly engage in it. Using all five senses to imagine their favorite place may present a challenge to adults facing a myriad of other tasks each day. Many adults want to use an anxiety-reducing strategy for the first time when they are experiencing anxiety. However, if the individual can work first to define their favorite place when they are not feeling anxious, they can better utilize the imagery when they are actually anxious. Other adults may struggle to fully develop a mental visualization of their favorite place. If this is the case, they may benefit from listening to a script to guide them through an imagery exercise. They can choose to listen to the script when they are feeling anxious or memorize the script so that it can be replayed in their heads at any time. These strategies will not be effective for all adults with anxiety; it is encouraged for the individual to practice the strategy to determine if they find it to be effective in decreasing their anxiety before they actually need it.

Desk Yoga/Stretching

Yoga is an ancient Hindu discipline, which has been around for over 5000 years. It is the practice of body postures, meditation and breathing control. Stretching is a form of physical exercise where a specific muscle is flexed or stretched. Both techniques are proven to reduce stress and tension and improve concentration and focus.

Students who experience anxiety normally experience tense muscles. Muscles tend to tighten up in response to physical and emotional stress. By transferring focus and attention from anxious feelings and emotions to the body and breath, these techniques can address anxiety while also releasing physical tension.

Students can perform the following techniques in the classroom without attracting attention or interrupting instruction:

Camel Pose
Sit in a chair with your feet flat on the ground and your knees together. Lift your head, open your chest, squeeze your shoulder blades together, and place your hands on the back of the chair. Gently press your hips forward while shifting your shoulders back, slowly arching your back. Look up, keeping your spine neutral.

Shoulder Shrug
Sit or stand with your arms at your side. Gently shrug your shoulders up toward your ears. Hold for 30 seconds. Gently release your shoulders until your arms are hanging normally at your sides. Repeat at least three times.

Cat Pose
From a sitting position with your feet flat on the ground, round your back and tuck your chin into your chest, stretching your back.

Shoulder Rolls
Back Shoulder Roll: Sit or stand with your arms at your side. Gently shrug your shoulders up toward your ears. Slowly roll your shoulders back and down as you release the shrug. Repeat three times.
Front Shoulder Roll: Continue by shrugging your shoulders up toward your ears. Slowly roll your shoulders forward and down as you release the shrug. Repeat three times.

Pigeon Pose
Sit tall with your feet flat on the ground. Bend your right leg and place your right ankle on your left knee. Place your left hand on your right foot and your right hand on your right knee. Apply light pressure on your right knee. Switch sides and repeat the steps.

Back/Side Stretch
Interlace your fingers and push your hands away from your body. Gently stretch your arms up over your head. Gently lean to the left and hold for 30 seconds. Then gently lean to the right and hold for 30 seconds. Repeat three times.
Interlace fingers behind your back. If you can't interlace your fingers in the back, just keep your fingers and arms outstretched behind you. Gently stretch and hold this for 30 seconds. Repeat three times.

Seated Twist

Sit upright in your chair. Check that your spine is straight and your feet are flat on the ground. Twist your upper body to the right. Place your left hand on your right knee and your right hand on the back of the chair. Gently twist toward the back of the chair. Repeat on the other side.

Wrist Stretch

Hold your right arm straight out in front of you with your fingers to the sky – like you are signaling STOP. Take your left hand and gently pull your right fingers back toward your chest. Hold for thirty seconds. Repeat on the other arm.

Cobra Pose

Come to sit at the front of your chair. Open your chest, squeeze your shoulder blades together, look up, and bring your hands to the back of the chair. Arch into a baby back bend.

Extended Side Angle Pose

Sit toward the front of your chair with your feet flat on the ground and your legs and feet together. Tilt your upper body forward, then twist to the right, rest your left elbow on your right knee, lengthening your left hand toward the ground. Look up and reach your right arm straight up to the sky. Repeat on the other side.

Grade-Level Implementation

Desk yoga and stretching are fun strategies to use for reducing anxiety. It works best with younger students and adults; they are not as fearful about other people's reactions when using this strategy. Desk yoga can be practiced anywhere with or without a chair, so school counselors will need to consult with the classroom teacher before allowing a student to use this strategy in the classroom. This strategy is also popular among students with anxiety because it can be used as an effective tool for preventing anxiety.

Elementary School

Elementary school students are known for their high levels of activeness both in and out of the classroom. Desk yoga and stretching can work successfully with all young students – especially those with anxiety. It can relax and soothe their bodies, which in turn works to soothe their minds. Their bodies relay calming information to the brain, which tells them everything is ok. This slows their heart rates and lowers their blood pressure, which lowers anxiety levels. It can also be used as a preventative strategy when they feel their anxiety levels increasing.

Desk yoga strategies can be taught to individual students, small counseling groups or entire classes. With the variety of exercises available, elementary school students can try numerous desk yoga strategies to determine three to five that are most effective for them. While desk yoga can be a fun activity, young students need to find the exercises that work to decrease their anxiety. Some of the exercises may be enjoyable but ineffective at reducing anxiety. Therefore, it is important that the school counselor assists students in understanding the difference between effective/ineffective desk yoga exercises. When using desk yoga and stretching with small counseling groups or entire classes, the school counselor must guide students into understanding which exercises work for them. Elementary students who learn to manage anxiety at young ages can benefit by growing their confidence and increasing their feelings of well-being. School counselors will need to be certain the classroom teacher understands what the student is doing since many young students may naturally move around a lot in their chairs.

Middle/Junior High School

Students in the middle/junior high school setting can also benefit from using desk yoga and stretching to lower their anxiety levels. Although these students are expected to be more focused and still than their elementary counterparts, most are still excited to have the opportunity to move around in their chairs. The self-consciousness that typically prevents some middle/junior high school students from participating in physical activities is not as evident when they get to engage in desk yoga exercises. Meditation or imagery may be too challenging for some middle/junior high school students with anxiety, whereas desk yoga and stretching may be more appropriate as they do not require as much intensity and focus. Sitting at a desk most of the day can increase some students' anxieties; having the chance to move around can ease some of that for middle/junior high school students.

The only tool that may be needed for these strategies is a chair and/or desk. Since these are readily available to students, this strategy can be helpful in the classroom. School counselors can walk an entire class through different desk yoga exercises and assist them in finding which exercise works best for them. If an anxious middle/junior high school student is using desk yoga exercises individually in the classroom, they may consider using some of the exercises that draw less attention to themselves. It does not serve the purpose of decreasing anxiety if they feel anxious about using the desk yoga exercises. Some of the arm, neck, hand and leg exercises may be more practical and subtle for students to use. However, if they are comfortable using more active desk yoga strategies to lower their anxiety levels and the teacher allows it, they have a wider variety of exercises from which to choose.

High School

Teenagers are exceptionally good at finding ways to move around in their desks at school. Desk yoga bridges the gap between randomly moving around in their seats and intentionally moving to serve a purpose. Teachers must be on board with students using this strategy as it can become a distraction to others in the classroom if not used appropriately. For an anxious high school student, being able to use desk yoga and stretching exercises can help relieve some of their nervous energy that has built up during the school day to reduce their anxiety levels. Desk yoga can also contribute to better health for high school students by lowering their heart rate and allowing them to focus on better breathing habits.

In order to prevent any potential health problems or injuries, the school counselor should check with the student to make sure they don't have any physical limitations that could prevent them from using desk yoga or stretching exercises.

School counselors can work individually with students to consider each of their classes and which ones increase their anxiety. After this has been established, the school counselor can teach students several desk yoga and stretching exercises to help the student determine which exercises are effective. High school students may find different desk yoga exercises will yield different results for them, sometimes in different classes.

Once a student determines which exercises will work for them, they can talk to their teachers with the school counselor present to explain why and what they will be doing in their seats during times of increased anxiety. Once the teachers understand why the student will be intentionally moving around in their desks, the student can begin to use desk yoga as a means for decreasing their anxiety.

Post-Secondary

While at work and in college, adults are faced with many stressful situations that can be detrimental to their health. Although it is a helpful tool for handling stress, many adults will report a lack of time for why they don't engage in yoga or any type of exercise. Many adults use yoga as a tool for creating better health and balance in their lives. Desk yoga can serve many purposes to college students and other adults since it provides physical as well as mental benefits. As they use desk yoga, they may find it provides health benefits such as lowering blood pressure and heart rate, stretching tight muscles and increasing blood flow. Mental benefits for adults include a decrease in anxiety, better focus, and a clearer mind.

Whether at home, in an office, or in a dorm room, most adults have access to a chair. All that is needed to use desk yoga as a strategy for anxiety reduction is a chair/desk and the adult's willingness to fully engage in the exercise. No lengthy time commitment is involved, so this strategy can be easily utilized by an extremely busy yet anxious person. In determining which desk yoga exercises work best, adults and college students need to examine where their anxiety levels are the highest. Adults can then choose five or more different desk yoga exercises to utilize during those anxious times. They may find different desk yoga exercises work for different parts of their day, so they will have to individualize a plan that works best for them. Adults and college students can then use desk yoga as often as they need to help lower their anxiety levels.

Progressive Muscle Relaxation

Progressive muscle relaxation is a technique that can relieve muscle tension associated with anxiety. Practicing progressive muscle relaxation involves tensing a group of muscles while inhaling, and relaxing them while exhaling. Teaching students to progress through muscle groups from their head to their feet can lead to total body relaxation. As the student works through each muscle group, they should consider: How does this body part feel? Is it cold or warm, tight or relaxed? If there is tightness or stress, imagine breathing the stress out of that part of the body with each exhale.

To practice progressive muscle relaxation with students, school counselors can lead students through the following:

Inhale, and tense the first muscle group for 4 to 10 seconds.
Exhale, and suddenly and completely relax the muscle group.
Notice the difference between how the muscles feel when they are tense and how they feel when they are relaxed.

Repeat with the next muscle group.

Muscle groups:	Action:
Forehead, eyes, nose	Raise eyebrows, squint eyes and wrinkle nose.
Cheeks and jaws	Smile widely.
Mouth	Press your lips together tightly.
Neck	Touch chin to chest.
Hands	Clench into fists.
Upper arms	Clench hands into fists, bend arms at the elbows, and flex biceps.
Shoulders	Raise shoulders toward ears.
Back	Arch up and away from the chair.
Stomach	Contract into a tight knot.
Hips and buttocks	Press buttocks together tightly.
Thighs	Clench hard.
Lower legs	Point toes toward face, then away, and curl them downward at the same time.

Grade-Level Implementation

Progressive muscle relaxation is one of the most useful strategies for lowering anxiety due to its discreet nature. Students with anxiety can use this strategy at their desks and no one will have any idea they are doing anything out of the ordinary. This strategy works well for all age levels. Everyone carries some type of muscle tension in their bodies, and progressive muscle relaxation allows students to relax their muscles, which reduces their anxiety levels.

Elementary School

Young students can learn to gain control of their bodies through the use of progressive muscle relaxation. Elementary students like to be physically active, so this strategy can be especially effective since it allows the student to move. Many young students with anxiety also appreciate the opportunity to move without other students knowing what they are doing. Elementary students are beginning to learn more about their bodies; this strategy allows them to start learning the difference between tense muscles and relaxed muscles. Students can learn to repeat progressive muscle relaxation as both a reactive and proactive strategy for lowering their anxiety. Also, if they master progressive muscle relaxation when they are young, it will be a tool they can use to help in reducing their anxiety for the rest of their lives.

While young students can't see the effect of progressive muscle relaxation on their bodies, they can feel the difference between tensing and relaxing their muscles. School counselors need to help elementary students to first understand what their bodies feel like when they are feeling anxiety. This helps the student become more self-aware of when they are carrying tension in their body due to their anxiety. Students need to learn to be specific about where in their body they are feeling anxiety. School counselors can then take the student through the progressive muscle relaxation exercise and allow them to tense and release the different muscle groups. If a student struggles to understand this concept, school counselors can use analogies to help them understand the difference between tense and relaxed, such as comparing a cooked and uncooked piece of spaghetti. The student can start from the top of their head and move through each muscle group while tensing and relaxing them. Elementary students respond well to using progressive muscle relaxation as a strategy for decreasing their anxiety.

Middle/Junior High School

Students in middle/junior high school find progressive muscle relaxation to be a preferred strategy due to the ability to use it discreetly. While many other strategies may bring some sort of attention to the student, this strategy can be implemented with no one else knowing. The student may not tense every muscle group, such a grinning as widely as they can, but rather tense the muscle groups that will not draw attention. When they practice progressive muscle relaxation, they will find the strategy comes more easily to them. Over time they may start to notice a positive difference in their anxiety levels.

When starting to introduce progressive muscle relaxation to a middle/junior high school student, the school counselor may first have to help the student identify different muscle groups in the body. Once those are better understood by the student, they can learn to tense and relax each of those muscle groups. One key for this strategy to be successful is for the student to work on this skill during times of calm. This allows them to automatically use it when their anxiety is increasing without having to think about how to implement it. After the student gets used to using progressive muscle relaxation, the school counselor can work with them to identify which areas of their body carries their anxiety. The student can then focus specifically on tensing and relaxing that muscle group. If working through this with the school counselor increases the student's anxiety, they can also choose to listen to a script that leads them through progressive muscle relaxation. The middle/junior high school student may also elect to use other strategies for reducing their anxiety levels.

High School

When teenagers with anxiety carry tension in their bodies, it can negatively impact other areas of their lives. They may struggle to sleep, experience headaches from constantly tensing up their necks and shoulders, clench their jaws and have backaches from tensing up back muscles when anxious. High school students may not understand carrying around this tension is actually increasing their anxiety. They don't always realize the tense muscles in their bodies are due to anxiety and instead attribute it to other factors. Progressive muscle relaxation is a helpful strategy that will teach teenagers to identify where they carry their tension in their bodies and how to reduce it.

Post-Secondary

Some adults with anxiety have carried around tension in their bodies for so long that they don't know what it feels like to *not* have tension in their bodies. It's a struggle for them to relax because they have forgotten what that feels like in their bodies. The health consequences of carrying tension around in their bodies can be long term and serious. It could result in heart disease, high blood pressure, migraines and sleeping problems. Progressive muscle relaxation allows an adult to feel the tightening and relaxing of their muscles. It can be used every day as a proactive strategy to decrease their anxiety and better their physical health.

For anxious adults and college students who have not experienced muscle relaxation in a long time, they will need to relearn how it feels to deeply relax the muscles in their bodies. After training their bodies to feel the difference between tension and relaxation in their muscles, they need to systematically use progressive muscle relaxation to release the tension in their muscles. As they learn to tense and relax their muscles, it is important that they identify which muscle groups carry the most anxiety in their bodies. Just as with young students, college students and other adults can practice this strategy in any environment whether it's before a big exam, at work, in the car or at home. If they practice it often enough, adults can learn to automatically tense and release their muscles when they are feeling anxious without having to intentionally do so.

Printables and Trigger Trackers

Anxiety printables can be very useful in helping younger students identify their emotions and gain a better understanding of where their anxieties come from. Printables may also be a useful strategy for older students who benefit from seeing visual representations of their anxiety and/or coping strategies. Printables also have a multitude of uses for anxiety reduction. They can be used by students with anxiety for journaling, writing positive affirmations, drawing pictures, writing positive self-talk quotes and list breathing exercises. Using trigger trackers allows students with anxiety to better identify what triggers their anxiety. Older students may benefit more from utilizing this strategy since they may be better at noticing patterns in their behaviors. They may also better identify what triggers their anxiety and track how often those triggers are occurring in their daily lives.

There are a multitude of creative and fun printables school counselors can use with students to address anxiety. Information sheets, worksheets, and coloring pages can be found pertaining to coping skills, cognitive distraction techniques, deep breathing, exercises to relieve anxiety, cognitive restructuring etc. These tangible documents can be a concrete reminder of coping strategies.

How different strategies can be used with students in different school settings is explained below – to help them work through anxiety both in and out of the school setting.

Grade-Level Implementation

Elementary School

Even with technology's more prominent role in learning, students in elementary school settings are still very accustomed to receiving handouts in order to complete their school work. Many students learn better when they have an actual piece of paper in front of them. Elementary school students with anxiety can benefit from using printables as a means of helping to reduce anxiety. Being able to actively work through their negative thoughts and feelings on paper can help them process their anxiety and learn better ways to cope. While there are a multitude of printables available for students with anxiety, some may be of more interest than others to students.

School counselors can find a great number of free printables available online or can develop their own for students. Elementary students can work with their school counselors to determine which printables will be the most helpful in decreasing their anxiety. Some students may prefer to write about their anxiety while others may prefer a printable that only requires them to answer with words or short sentences. Other young students may prefer checking off their emotions on a printable or drawing a picture that helps explain what they are feeling when they have anxiety. While older students may experience better success with identifying their triggers, elementary students may still benefit from completing a printed checklist that helps them narrow down what causes their anxiety. Although many students like to draw or write about their anxiety on a printable sheet, some appreciate a printable with reminders for ways to help with their anxiety. Some sheets may list out ways to help with their anxiety, while others may have visuals or phrases that can serve as reminders in how they can work to lower their anxiety.

Middle/Junior High School

For some middle/junior high school students, completing a printable may seem childish. For others, they welcome the opportunity to write or draw about their anxiety on a printable instead of explaining it out loud. Students in middle/junior high school start to have a better understanding of what triggers their anxiety than elementary school students. Printables that list a number of possible anxiety triggers can assist them in pinpointing what triggers their anxiety. Other printables may help them identify when their anxiety triggers will happen. Gaining self-awareness through these strategies can prove helpful in working to decrease their anxiety.

School counselors need to work one on one with middle/junior high school students to determine if using printables and/or trigger trackers will be a helpful strategy in lowering their anxiety. As they get to know themselves better, some middle/junior high school students find charting out their triggers over a few weeks enables them to learn more about themselves and their emotions. If they aren't comfortable charting their triggers, the student can work with their school counselor to choose other strategies that are more useful. Some middle/junior high school students find using printables helps them discover more about their emotions and challenge their negative thoughts. Helpful examples of positive coping skills on a printable may assist students to remember strategies when they see it. Being able to break down their negative thoughts on paper can help challenge their previous thinking about their anxiety. While printables and trigger trackers don't work for all middle/junior high school students, the majority of them can find one type of printable that aids them in better understanding their anxiety.

High School

Older students in high school have a higher ability to identify emotions. Using printables that list different anxiety triggers can be very effective for helping students understand what specifically triggers their anxiety. Understanding when it happens can also help pinpoint ways to help decrease it. Many high school students with anxiety like to write or draw; different printables allow them to engage in either activity while working to ease their anxiety. Other printables may illustrate different strategies for dealing with their anxiety.

Although many students like to journal, some high school students who don't like to write will enjoy printables because of their succinctness. Filling in the blanks or checking off triggers on a list can be preferable for some students who don't like to write or talk about their anxiety. School counselors can work with high school students to choose which printables are most helpful in decreasing their anxiety. Some printables may allow the high school student to write out a plan for which positive strategies they will use when they are experiencing anxiety. Additional printables can be utilized to aid in identifying specific anxiety-reducing strategies for different triggers. These might include how to lower their anxiety before a test, giving a presentation in class, attending school, trying to speak to someone else, manage panic attacks, when getting swept up in social media, etc. High school students can try many different printables and use the ones that are most effective in helping them lower their anxiety.

Post-Secondary

College students and adults may not utilize printables and trigger trackers in the same ways as students in the K-12 setting. They may be more likely to use a printable in the format of a journal, diary or adult coloring book. In addition, some may prefer to use an online tool. Many trigger trackers are available online along with apps for phones. College students and adults may be more apt to use these if they prefer to utilize technology. Other adults want a tangible item as they work to identify and work to reduce their anxiety. There are an abundance of printables adults may choose to use as encouragement for when they are feeling anxious. There are quotes and pictures that may be printed and placed where they can be seen daily by the individual. Adults may also use printables to list goals for decreasing their anxiety. They may need printables with reminders of different strategies and how to use them. The individual college student or adult can determine which type of printables and/or trigger trackers are most useful in helping decrease their anxiety.

Conclusion

Anxiety does not limit itself to a particular age or developmental level and no two individuals experience it in the exact same way. Students in elementary, middle/junior high and high school experience anxiety in their own ways. Adults can encounter their anxiety in similar ways as they did when they were younger, or they may not even experience anxiety until adulthood. Different anxiety reduction strategies work differently for different individuals. Some may find that many different strategies work in reducing their anxiety. Others may find that only a few strategies are effective for them. As they discover which strategies work best for them, they can begin to implement them into their daily lives. This will allow the strategies to be used in both a reactive and proactive manner, potentially preventing some future anxiety from occurring. Once a student or adult determines the most useful strategies, they can implement them into their anxiety survival toolkit that will be discussed later in this book.

I'm working with my school counselor to learn some strategies for how to handle my anxiety. It's hard, because I want to just run away from everything when my anxiety goes into high gear. But I have to remember to use the techniques she taught me. I am trying to use the deep breathing before I take a test. When I feel my body start to tense up like I'm going to have a panic attack, I'm going to try to use the cognitive distraction strategy and start counting how many blue things I see in the room. If that doesn't work, then I'm going to close my eyes for fifteen seconds and count how many sounds I can hear around me so that it will distract my mind from my anxiety. I tried it in her office and it worked! I hope it will work in the classroom, too.

– Anxious Annie

7 What Goes in the Anxiety Survival Toolkit

I need something to help me with my anxiety. When I'm sitting in class and having a meltdown in my head, I wish I knew how to talk myself out of having a panic attack. I wish I knew how to get myself calm and not feel like I'm having a heart attack. I want to have more good days than bad days, and I want to learn how to get some control of myself and my life. I want my anxiety to stop controlling me and get in control of myself. I know my school counselor taught me some strategies, but I don't always remember them when I'm sitting in the classroom feeling like a panic attack is coming on.

– Anxious Annie

Introduction

The primary goal of a school counselor is to increase academic achievement. The best way for school counselors to increase academic achievement is to have students in class, ready to learn. Arming students with techniques to address anxiety that can be used in the classroom can reduce lost instructional time, empower the student to manage their anxiety and increase academic achievement.

The key to stopping anxiety symptoms is an understanding of WHY and WHAT and to have a plan ready to stop the negative thoughts and emotions as they start. The ability to stop the spiraling negative thoughts is key, and when students have preplanned interventions they know how to use there is a greater chance of success.

Often, when students experience anxiety, they are so caught up in the negative thoughts and emotions, they forget what strategies to use to manage their anxiety (Goldstein, n.d.). Creating an anxiety survival toolkit for students gathers the interventions and techniques that work into a tangible, portable and nondescript toolkit they can use anytime, anywhere. Having access to their anxiety survival toolkit will remind them why they are experiencing anxiety, what basic need they are trying to satisfy and how to stop the negative thoughts.

The ultimate goal is to have students using their anxiety survival toolkits to help them suppress their flight response and stay in the classroom. Flight is a common response for students with anxiety. However, escaping the environment causing anxiety will counterintuitively make it worse. In fact, it can lead to students relying on some type of behavioral or cognitive avoidance. To successfully address anxiety, students must learn and use strategies to manage their emotions, thoughts and negative feelings as they occur. Even if a student needs to divert their attention away from instruction for a few minutes to address their anxiety, they will have the ability to refocus their mind and rejoin instruction much sooner than if they had to leave the classroom. This leads to increased instructional time, which correlates to increased academic achievement.

Individualizing the Anxiety Survival Toolkit for Students

Anxiety survival toolkits are tangible ways to remind students of their WHY, WHAT and HOW when they are experiencing anxiety. This toolkit can help students pause their negative thoughts, implement a strategy they know will work and refocus their attention.

Counselors should look for creative ways to personalize anxiety survival toolkits for each student. The toolkits can be stored in notebooks, folders, on a single sheet of paper or on electronic devices. The key is to store the toolkit where the student is comfortable accessing it and where it will not draw attention to itself when the student uses it. For example, if electronic devices are not allowed in the classroom, the student's anxiety survival toolkit needs to be stored elsewhere. Also, if a student is uncomfortable retrieving a notebook during class because it will draw attention, they may opt for a single sheet of paper.

Another important consideration when designing the anxiety survival toolkit is the environment where the student will use it. If the environment is a particular classroom, counselors should work with the teacher to design a toolkit that is effective in their class. If the student has most of their anxiety in the hallways, an electronic device may be warranted. And in special circumstances, the student may need more than one type of anxiety survival toolkit. For example, they may need a notebook to use during class, but prefer a single sheet of paper to use on the bus.

Before the anxiety survival toolkit can be assembled, the student must find their WHY and WHAT (chapter 5). In addition, the counselor should introduce all the HOWS (chapter 6) to determine which strategies work for the student. Once this groundwork is laid, an effective toolkit can be assembled.

Assembling the Anxiety Survival ToolKit

The first item that goes into the student's anxiety survival toolkit is their WHY. The school counselor should retrieve the 5 Why activity completed with the student and have them write their 5 WHYs on the first page of their notebook. If the toolkit will be stored electronically, look for ways to upload a picture of their handwritten 5 Whys, or have the student type it in a prominent place. At the end of the 5 Whys, have the student bold, underline or highlight their final WHY.

The second item in the anxiety survival toolkit is the student's WHAT. The school counselor should have the student write WHAT basic need they are trying to meet and bold, underline or highlight the identified basic need. Then have the student write their Reason Statement and bold, underline or highlight their Reason Statement.

It is important for the student to write, in their handwriting, their WHY and WHAT. Writing enables the student to personally connect with their statements and helps reinforce their meanings. If the student's toolkit is electronic, look for ways to upload the student's written statements.

The next step in assembling a student's anxiety survival toolkit is to select three to five strategies the student finds helpful to counteract their anxiety. These strategies can be selected from chapter 6, or from other strategies the student finds helpful. The toolkit's primary purpose is to help students stop the spiraling emotions associated with anxiety, so the ease of access to these strategies is vital. Therefore, how the strategies are presented will depend on the type of anxiety survival toolkit the student will use.

Notebook Anxiety Survival Toolkits

There are several types of notebooks that can be used. Composition notebooks, spiral bound notebooks and novelty notebooks all work well to construct an anxiety survival toolkit. Creative counselors and/or students can create notebooks from scratch to add additional personal touches. The notebook can be as elaborate or ordinary as the student desires.

The first page will be the student's hand written WHY, WHAT and Reason Statement. The following pages will have the strategies chosen by the student. Depending on the strategies chosen, the student can write, draw, glue or insert the strategies into their anxiety survival toolkit. The remainder of the toolkit has paper for the student to journal, record triggers and/or draw.

After the WHY, WHAT and Reason Statement have been placed prominently into the Anxiety Survival Toolkit, the strategies selected by the student are inserted. These can be written, glued or drawn by the student.

Single Paper Anxiety Survival Toolkits

Students may choose to have a much smaller toolkit or one that can be stored in a pocket or in their ID badge. This presents the unique problem of getting all the information on a single piece of paper. The benefit of this type of toolkit is it can be a succinct, no-nonsense way to address their anxiety.

The hand written WHY, WHAT and Reason Statement should always be in a prevalent place on the paper. The HOWs can either be written or the student can use symbols to remind them of the strategies. For example, writing 4-7-8 can remind the student to use the 4-7-8 breathing technique, *or* the word "count" can remind the student to use a cognitive distraction technique.

Folder and Binder Anxiety Survival Toolkits

Folder and Binder toolkits allow the student to easily add and remove items. This can be especially helpful as the student grows in their ability to manage anxiety. This type of anxiety survival toolkit is also beneficial when the student needs the ability to journal, uses printables or needs a more extensive explanation of how to use their HOWs.

The first page will have the student's hand written WHY, WHAT and Reason Statement. The following pages will have the strategies chosen by the student. Depending on the strategies chosen, the student can write, draw or insert the strategies into their toolkit. Be sure the toolkit has plenty of paper for the student to journal, record triggers and/or draw.

Electronic Anxiety Survival Toolkits

Electronic toolkits can be stored on any device the student uses. These anxiety survival toolkits work well with digital natives who view electronics as an extension of themselves. And as preteen and teenagers are never without their phones, these students will never be without their anxiety survival toolkit.

There are several ways to store an electronic anxiety survival toolkit. It can be a collection of pictures, an epub, an app or on any platform that the student is comfortable using. This will be dependent on what type of electronic device that will be used (phones, tablets, laptops, desktops, etc.).

Conclusion

When students have a plan to address their anxiety, they become prepared, empowered and armed with proven strategies they know will make a difference. This knowledge helps students remain calm, stay in the classroom and successfully address their anxiety. Assisting students in creating their anxiety survival toolkits may be one of the greatest gifts school counselors can give their students.

I have my own anxiety survival toolkit! I told my school counselor that I was having trouble remembering the strategies she taught me to use for when I start to feel my anxiety getting bad, and she helped me put together a notebook that she called my very own personal Annie's anxiety survival toolkit. It's a composition notebook with a pocket on the inside. I put a picture of my dog Charlie in the pocket, because he's my best friend and it makes me feel better to see his sweet furry face. She also got me to write down some of the strategies that work for me, like looking around and noticing all of the red things in the classroom. I also wrote down some of my favorite positive quotes that help me feel strong so I can read them when I need to. And I love to draw, so there are blank pages for that, too. She also talked to my teachers so that they know what my anxiety survival toolkit is and how I'll use it— that way I won't get in trouble in class for taking it out and using it. This is going to help me so much in class!

— Anxious Annie

8 Anxiety Survival Toolkit Use in Small Counseling Groups and School Counseling Classroom Lessons

I've always felt like I'm the only person that feels this way, but then my school counselor asked me to be in a small counseling group with other students who have anxiety. I didn't know there were other kids in the school that feels like I do—I thought I was the only anxious one out there! I'm really scared about telling other students about my anxiety, but I guess since we're all anxious they'll be just as scared as me.

– Anxious Annie

Introduction

Students can benefit from creating their own anxiety survival toolkit to have in the school setting. While these are best created individually with the student and school counselor, they can also be constructed in small counseling groups or in a school counseling classroom lesson. There is a vast array of small group and school counseling classroom lessons available to help students learn to manage their anxiety. These resources can be found on the internet and in professional resource books. Additionally, numerous children's books on topics involving anxiety, worry and stress are available for working with students. School counselors can use these resources to create intentional and successful lessons based on the needs and developmental levels of their students. Furthermore, they can implement the creation of the anxiety survival toolkit into these lessons, which will provide each student with their own unique set of tools for alleviating their anxiety.

Small Counseling Groups

Due to developmental and age differences, school counselors need to determine the most appropriate type of small counseling group to assemble. Depending on students' types of anxieties, the school counselor should consider how to best group students and focus the lessons for the small group. To find participants for a small counseling group that will teach anxiety reducing strategies, school counselors can reach out to teachers, parents, other school counselors in the building and/or let students self-nominate. They could also consult their counseling logs to search for students who frequently visit due to their anxiety. These students may be ideal candidates for a small counseling group due to their repeated visits to the school counselor's office. As the school counselor considers possible small group participants, they should screen potential members to make certain that they are selecting students open to changing their behaviors.

The goal of the small counseling group for anxiety is not to completely eliminate anxiety but rather to help students learn appropriate ways to manage it (Truluck, 2019). For students participating in a small counseling group for anxiety, it can be very empowering to know that their emotions are not strange or unique and that others want to help them with their anxiety. The small counseling group can enable them to gain support from their school counselor and peers. Additionally, students can help each other by sharing how anxiety reducing strategies work for them. When students observe their peers experiencing success with particular techniques, they may be more likely to try them for themselves. As school counselors plan for their small counseling group for anxiety, they will need to consider their students' ages and developmental levels. They should also plan for how they will assist students to create and use their anxiety survival toolkits.

One of the goals of the small counseling group will be to help students better understand and manage their anxiety. The school counselor will accomplish this task by not only teaching students different strategies to address their anxiety but also guiding them to create their personal anxiety survival toolkit. Small group counseling curriculum can include an assortment of activities that are tailored to the age of the students. The individual needs of the students are also important considerations; some students' anxiety levels may be more intense than others. If a student has extreme levels of anxiety, they may not be an appropriate fit for a small counseling group. That student may be better served by individual counseling; their interactions with other anxious students may only increase their own anxiety. Depending on the age level of the students, the school counselor may choose to incorporate more hands-on activities, those that integrate deeper discussion or activities that require movement.

There are a number of tools a school counselor can use when working with their anxiety small counseling group. One effective tool many school counselors use for small groups is children's books. All students, no matter their age, enjoy hearing a good story. School counselors can choose to incorporate a children's book about anxiety into each/some of their small counseling group sessions. The following children's books provide relevant and interesting stories that resonate with anxious students:

- *A Little SPOT of Anxiety: A Story about Calming Your Worries* by Diane Alber
- *All Birds Have Anxiety* by Kathy Hoopmann
- *Anxious Ninja* by Mary Nhin
- *David and the Worry Beast: Helping Children Cope With Anxiety* by Anne Marie Guanci
- *How Big Are Your Worries Little Bear?* by Jayneen Sanders
- *Wemberly Worried* by Kevin Henkes
- *Wilma Jean the Worry Machine* by Julia Cook
- *Worry Says What?* by Allison Edwards

Other tools for an anxiety small counseling group include individual composition notebooks and supplies for coloring, cutting, gluing and decorating. Group members will use these supplies to create and individualize their anxiety survival tool kit. School counselors should also provide relaxing music and have the availability to access technology.

In addition to showing students how to effectively use their anxiety survival toolkit, the school counselor may also choose to show students free apps that are available to help with their anxiety. As technology moves and changes quickly, different videos and apps may be available to the school counselor. A simple search of the word "anxiety" or "calm" will yield dozens of free apps that can be downloaded and used by students. Video clips may be a valuable medium to teach students how to manage their anxiety. School counselors should emphasize that videos and apps do not replace human interactions and are one of many strategies accessible for use by students with anxiety.

Before creating a small counseling group curriculum, school counselors will need to consider the particular focus of the group. While anxiety comes in many different forms, the strategies used by school counselors to work with each form are very similar. Many students have test anxiety, so the small counseling group may emphasize this particular type of anxiety in its curriculum. Other students may exhibit high levels of worry, so the small counseling group may focus on that topic. In addition to determining the focus of the small counseling group, coming up with a group name can aid the school counselor in attracting more participants. Catchy names tend to work with younger students, such as "Stress Busters" or "Worry Warriors." Older students may prefer names that are both simple and direct, such as the "Dealing with Anxiety" group. The number of group meetings may need to be flexible, depending on how frequently the school counselor can pull students from their classes. Facilitating eight small group sessions is ideal, but many school counselors may only be able to integrate six lessons into their anxiety small counseling group.

School counselors can employ similar activities they use in other small counseling groups into the anxiety group curriculum. They will use getting to know you activities along with icebreaker activities in order to help group participants know and become more comfortable around each other. It will be necessary to modify these activities as needed to meet the diverse needs of their group members. As most students with anxiety feel a lack of control in their lives, it will be crucial for the school counselor to establish a structure for each of their small counseling group sessions. Beginning each session the same way can create a sense of calm and control with the group members. Similarly, ending each session with the same activity allows students to feel relaxed and at ease when returning back to class after the session. Furthermore, the setting in which the small group counseling takes places should be one that provides privacy to the group members. Some students may not want others outside of the group to know they are struggling with anxiety. A private environment will also allow students to try different anxiety reducing strategies without the self-consciousness they experience when others are watching.

Below is a sample template for creating a small counseling group for students with anxiety. This template can be modified to meet the needs of the school counselor's particular small group. Please keep in mind different ages and developmental levels will affect the efficacy of some activities. Additionally, the term "Level Specific" will be listed to specify modifications needed for elementary, middle/junior high or high school. If the school counselor can only complete six small group counseling sessions with students, sessions five and seven may be combined with session four and six in order to teach all of the anxiety reduction strategies.

Session One

Supplies Needed

- Large paper for listing group rules, composition notebooks, glue, scissors, construction paper/magazines, crayons/markers, items for decorating notebooks, yoga mats, relaxing music, dry erase board (optional).
- Level Specific: any supplies needed for getting to know you and icebreaker activities.

Opening

- School counselor will play relaxing instrumental music in the background, share the purpose of the small counseling group, discuss confidentiality and the group meeting schedule.
- Group members will create rules for the small group.

Warm Up

- Level Specific: Getting to know you activity.
- Level Specific: Icebreaker activity.

Discussion

- School counselor and group members will discuss what anxiety is and how it feels for different people. This can take place as a verbal discussion or students can list feelings on a dry erase board.
- School counselor will share information about who gets anxiety and the reasons anxiety can develop. Older group members may benefit from hearing statistics about how many teenagers have been diagnosed with anxiety.
- School counselor will share general information about the coping strategies the group members will learn during small group counseling sessions.
- School counselor will share with the group what an anxiety survival toolkit is and how it can be used.

Activity

- Group members will each be given a composition notebook.
- School counselor will show an example of an anonymous student's anxiety survival toolkit and discuss how each session will include different strategies for dealing with anxiety.
- Group members will personalize the outside of their composition notebooks in order to turn them into individualized anxiety survival tool kits.

Some group members, particularly older group members, may elect to minimally decorate or not decorate the outside of their toolkit. They may want their anxiety survival toolkit to be used discreetly and have it appear as a normal composition notebook to their peers. It is the group member's choice to decorate it or not.

Debrief

- School counselor and group members will discuss how they feel about being in the group.
- School counselor and group members will discuss any fears or concerns they have about the group.
- Group members will discuss what they would like to get out of their participation in the small counseling group.

Wrap Up

- School counselor will remind group members about the confidentiality of the small group, how many meetings are left and the date/time of the next meeting.

- Group members will sit/lie on the floor on yoga mats (if available), close their eyes and listen to relaxing instrumental music until dismissal to return to class.

Session Two

Supplies Needed

- List of group rules, group members' anxiety survival toolkits, yoga mats, relaxing music.
- Level Specific: any supplies needed for getting to know you and icebreaker activities.
- Level Specific: children's book.

Opening

- School counselor will play relaxing instrumental music in the background, remind students about the purpose of the small counseling group, discuss confidentiality and the group meeting schedule.
- Group members will go over rules for the small group created in session one.

Warm Up

- Circle: Group members will sit in a circle (as space allows) and share what is currently contributing to their anxiety—school, home, family, friends, etc.
- Level Specific: School counselor will read a children's book about anxiety to group members.

Discussion

- Group members will discuss their reactions to the book and how it relates to their anxiety.
- School counselor and group members will discuss how their bodies feel when they are anxious.

Activity

- School counselor will teach students the following strategies to relieve anxiety: deep breathing techniques and progressive muscle relaxation.
- Group members will practice each strategy with each other and then on their own.
- Level Specific: School counselor will teach different deep breathing

techniques and progressive muscle relaxation strategies depending on the age of group members.

Debrief

– Group members will discuss how they felt before and after practicing deep breathing and progressive muscle relaxation.
– Group members will determine if the strategies presented are personally useful to reduce their anxiety. Useful strategies will be recorded in their anxiety survival toolkit.

Wrap Up

– School counselor will remind group members about the confidentiality of the small group, how many meetings are left and the date/time of the next meeting.
– Group members will sit/lie on the floor on yoga mats (if available), close their eyes and listen to relaxing instrumental music until dismissal to return to class.

Session Three

Supplies Needed

– List of group rules, group members' anxiety survival toolkits, yoga mats, relaxing music.

Opening

– School counselor will play relaxing instrumental music in the background, remind students about the purpose of the small counseling group, discuss confidentiality and the group meeting schedule.
– Group members will go over rules for the small group created in session one.

Warm Up

– Circle: Group members will sit in a circle (as space allows) and share what is currently contributing to their anxiety—school, home, family, friends, etc. Group members will then share any successes they've experienced in managing their anxiety.

Discussion

– School counselor will remind group members about deep breathing techniques and progressive muscle relaxation strategies learned in previous session. Refreshers will be shown as needed for group members.

- School counselor and group members will continue their discussion on how anxiety affects the body and the advantages of using desk yoga and stretching as anxiety relieving strategies. They will then discuss meditation and its use in reducing anxiety.

Activity

- School counselor will teach students the following strategies to relieve anxiety: desk yoga, stretching and meditation.
- Group members will practice each strategy with each other and then on their own.
- Level Specific: School counselor will teach different desk yoga, stretching and meditation strategies depending on the age of group members.

Debrief

- Group members will discuss how they felt before and after practicing desk yoga, stretching and meditation.
- Group members will determine if the strategies presented are personally useful to reduce their anxiety. Useful strategies will be recorded in their anxiety survival toolkit.

Wrap Up

- School counselor will remind group members about the confidentiality of the small group, how many meetings are left and the date/time of the next meeting.
- Group members will sit/lie on the floor on yoga mats (if available), close their eyes and listen to relaxing instrumental music until dismissal to return to class.

Session Four

Supplies Needed

- List of group rules, group members' anxiety survival toolkits, yoga mats, relaxing music.

Opening

- School counselor will play relaxing instrumental music in the

background, remind students about the purpose of the small counseling group, discuss confidentiality and the group meeting schedule.
– Group members will go over rules for the small group created in session one.

Warm Up

– Circle: Group members will sit in a circle (as space allows) and share what is currently contributing to their anxiety—school, home, family, friends, etc. Group members will then share any successes they've experienced in managing their anxiety.

Discussion

– School counselor will remind group members about desk yoga, stretching and meditation strategies learned in previous session. Refreshers will be shown as needed for group members.
– School counselor and group members will discuss negative thought patterns and how they increase anxiety. They will then discuss cognitive distraction, visualization and imagery and how they can be used in reducing anxiety.

Activity

– School counselor will teach students the following strategies to relieve anxiety: cognitive distraction, visualization and imagery.
– Group members will practice each strategy with each other and then on their own.
– Level Specific: School counselor will teach different cognitive distraction, visualization and imagery strategies depending on the age of group members.

Debrief

– Group members will discuss how they felt before and after practicing cognitive distraction, visualization and imagery.
– Group members will determine if the strategies presented are personally useful to reduce their anxiety. Useful strategies will be recorded in their anxiety survival toolkit.

Wrap Up

– School counselor will remind group members about the confidentiality

of the small group, how many meetings are left and the date/time of the next meeting.
-   Group members will sit/lie on the floor on yoga mats (if available), close their eyes and listen to relaxing instrumental music until dismissal to return to class.

Session Five (can be combined with Session Four if needed)

Supplies Needed

-   List of group rules, group members' anxiety survival toolkits, yoga mats, relaxing music, glue
-   Level Specific: printables and trigger tracker sheets.

Opening

-   School counselor will play relaxing instrumental music in the background, remind students about the purpose of the small counseling group, discuss confidentiality and the group meeting schedule.
-   Group members will go over rules for the small group created in session one.

Warm Up

-   Circle: Group members will sit in a circle (as space allows) and share what is currently contributing to their anxiety—school, home, family, friends, etc. Group members will then share any successes they've experienced in managing their anxiety.

Discussion

-   School counselor will remind group members about cognitive distraction, visualization and imagery strategies learned in previous session. Refreshers will be shown as needed for group members.
-   School counselor and group members will discuss printables (Level Specific) and trigger trackers. They will then discuss how printables and trigger trackers can be used to reduce and to track when they are experiencing anxiety.

Activity

-   School counselor will teach students the following strategies to relieve anxiety: printables and trigger trackers.
-   Group members will practice each strategy with each other and then on their own.

- Level Specific: School counselor will teach different printables and trigger tracker strategies depending on the age of group members.

Debrief

- Group members will discuss how they felt before and after practicing using printables and trigger trackers.
- Group members will determine if the strategies presented are personally useful to reduce their anxiety. Useful strategies will be recorded in their anxiety survival toolkit.

Wrap Up

- School counselor will remind group members about the confidentiality of the small group, how many meetings are left and the date/time of the next meeting.
- Group members will sit/lie on the floor on yoga mats (if available), close their eyes and listen to relaxing instrumental music until dismissal to return to class.

Session Six

Supplies Needed

- List of group rules, group members' anxiety survival toolkits, yoga mats, relaxing music, crayons/markers, glue.

Opening

- School counselor will play relaxing instrumental music in the background, remind students about the purpose of the small counseling group, discuss confidentiality and the group meeting schedule.
- Group members will go over rules for the small group created in session one.

Warm Up

- Circle: Group members will sit in a circle (as space allows) and share what is currently contributing to their anxiety—school, home, family, friends, etc. Group members will then share any successes they've experienced in managing their anxiety.

Discussion

- School counselor will remind group members about printables and

trigger tracker strategies learned in previous session. Refreshers will be shown as needed for group members.
- School counselor and group members will discuss journaling as a tool for reducing anxiety.

Activity

- School counselor will teach students the following strategy to relieve anxiety: journaling.
- Group members will practice this strategy with each other and then on their own.
- Level Specific: School counselor will teach different journaling strategies depending on the age and interest level of group members.

Debrief

- Group members will discuss how they felt before and after practicing journaling.
- Group members will determine if the strategies presented are personally useful to reduce their anxiety. Useful strategies will be recorded in their anxiety survival toolkit.

Wrap Up

- School counselor will remind group members about the confidentiality of the small group, how many meetings are left and the date/time of the next meeting.
- Group members will sit/lie on the floor on yoga mats (if available), close their eyes and listen to relaxing instrumental music until dismissal to return to class.

Session Seven (can be combined with Session Six if needed)

Supplies Needed

- List of group rules, group members' anxiety survival toolkits, yoga mats, relaxing music, glue, dry erase board (optional)
- Level Specific: age appropriate lists of positive self-talk and affirmations.

Opening

- School counselor will play relaxing instrumental music in the background, remind students about the purpose of the small counseling group, discuss confidentiality and the group meeting schedule.

– Group members will go over rules for the small group created in session one.

Warm Up

– Circle: Group members will sit in a circle (as space allows) and share what is currently contributing to their anxiety—school, home, family, friends, etc. Group members will then share any successes they've experienced in managing their anxiety.

Discussion

– School counselor will remind group members about journaling strategies learned in previous session. Refreshers will be shown as needed for group members.
– School counselor and group members will discuss positive self-talk and affirmations. School counselor will share how these strategies are similar and different. Small group will then discuss how positive self-talk and affirmations can be used to increase calm and self-esteem while alleviating anxiety. (Optional: group members can list positive self-talk and affirmations on dry erase board).

Activity

– School counselor will teach students the following strategies to relieve anxiety: positive self-talk and affirmations.
– Group members will practice each strategy with each other and then on their own. Group members may choose to create their own positive self-talk and affirmations.
– Level Specific: School counselor will teach different self-talk and affirmation strategies depending on the age of group members.

Debrief

– Group members will discuss how they felt before and after practicing positive self-talk and affirmations.
– Group members will determine if the strategies presented are personally useful to reduce their anxiety. Useful strategies will be recorded in their anxiety survival toolkit.

Wrap Up

– School counselor will remind group members about the confidentiality of the small group, how many meetings are left and the date/time of the next meeting.

- Group members will sit/lie on the floor on yoga mats (if available), close their eyes and listen to relaxing instrumental music until dismissal to return to class.

Session Eight

Supplies Needed

- List of group rules, group members' anxiety survival toolkits, yoga mats, relaxing music, snacks for celebration

Opening

- School counselor will play relaxing instrumental music in the background and share the successes of the small counseling group members.
- Group members will share their individual successes in learning to manage their anxiety.

Warm Up

- Circle: Group members will sit in a circle (as space allows) and share what is currently contributing to their anxiety—school, home, family, friends, etc. Group members will then share any successes they've experienced in managing their anxiety.

Discussion

- Each group member will complete a "show and tell" with their anxiety survival toolkit. They will share their anxiety survival toolkit components to group members.

Activity

- School counselor and group members will celebrate the conclusion of the small counseling group.

Debrief

- Group members will discuss their future plans to use their anxiety survival toolkits in order to alleviate their anxiety.

Wrap Up

- School counselor will remind group members about the confidentiality

of the small group and let them know that they will check in on them in the future.
–   Group members will sit/lie on the floor on yoga mats (if available), close their eyes and listen to relaxing instrumental music until dismissal to return to class.

After the conclusion of the last group session, the school counselor should follow up with group members and their teachers by completing check ins every couple of weeks to ask students how their anxiety levels are. School counselors can also check to make sure students are using their anxiety survival toolkits. A collaboration with teachers both before and after the small counseling group has ended will be helpful in preventing potential discipline concerns related to student's use of the anxiety survival toolkit. Students should not be fearful of using their anxiety survival toolkits in their classes for fear of getting in trouble.

The above session template has room for variation as needed. School counselors may also choose to incorporate a pre- and a posttest to determine the efficacy of the small anxiety group and anxiety levels of the students. Small counseling groups for anxiety can be varied in many different ways to meet the specific needs of the students in the school. There is no one right way for a school counselor to facilitate a small counseling group for anxiety with students.

School Counseling Classroom Lessons

Students of all ages are experiencing anxiety now more than ever. While some of these students know ways to advocate for themselves, others struggle to get the help they need. Some students don't realize they are experiencing anxiety, some don't understand how to ask for help and others may be too fearful to ask for help with dealing with their anxiety. When working with their student population, school counselors can employ different strategies for discerning which students are dealing with anxiety and need help. This may look different at different age levels for school counselors. For instance, a middle/junior or high school counselor may be able to e-mail their students or send out an electronic survey in order to gauge the need and interest in participating in a small counseling group for anxiety. An elementary school counselor may need to consult with teachers to determine participants for a small counseling group. However, despite different age levels, students at any age can benefit from improving their anxiety and stress levels. School counselors can share this information on a larger scale through school counseling classroom lessons.

Different schools have differing levels of support for how often a school counselor can facilitate a counseling classroom lesson with their students. While elementary school counselors may experience more success in accessing classrooms, gaining entry into classrooms in middle/junior and high school may present a significant challenge for the upper-level school counselor.

It becomes more difficult to reach a specific group of students as they begin to change teachers and move around the school more frequently than in elementary schools. School counselors at every level will need to collaborate with teachers to determine the best plan for utilizing counseling classroom lessons for working with students. Additionally, school counselors may consider speaking to teachers individually about what the lesson entails. They can provide data showing the importance of addressing stress/anxiety, which demonstrate the need for the lessons. The lessons can also be framed around an area of concern for many students, such as test anxiety in order to gain buy-in from teachers.

An ideal set of counseling classroom lessons on student anxiety would allow the school counselor to complete the lessons over the course of three classroom visits. This allows the school counselor to break down stress and anxiety for students and assist them in creating an individual stress/anxiety survival toolkit. Connecting the counseling classroom lesson with teaching standards can help create a collaborative relationship between the school counselor and classroom teacher. This may also help the school counselor present in the classroom more than once for this topic. On the other hand, some school counselors may only get one or two opportunities to present this lesson to a classroom. If this is the case, modifications can be made to the counseling classroom lessons in order to keep the lesson effective.

Using the word anxiety to describe students' struggles may be concerning to some students and teachers. Furthermore, school counselors cannot and should not be diagnosing students. However, when framed with experiencing stress, students and teachers will be more accepting of the topic. Therefore, counseling classroom lessons should be framed using the term "stress" instead of "anxiety." Students may choose to express they are experiencing anxiety, but for the sake of the counseling classroom lessons, the school counselor will experience better success in discussing stress. The end of the lessons will still result in students creating their own toolkits; their focus will be geared toward student stress rather than student anxiety.

Below is a sample template for creating a set of three counseling classroom lessons about dealing with stress for students. This template can be modified to meet the needs of the school counselor's particular classroom. Please keep in mind different ages and developmental levels will affect the efficacy of some activities. Additionally, the term "Level Specific" will be listed to specify modifications needed for work in elementary, middle/junior high or high school. If the school counselor can only complete one or two counseling classroom lessons with students, lessons two and/or three may be combined with lesson one in order to teach all of the stress reduction strategies. These school counseling classroom lesson plans can be tailored as necessary by the school counselor.

Lesson One

Title of Lesson

How to De-Stress Our Bodies

Objectives

- Define stress.
- Explain the difference between good stress and bad stress.
- Discuss how stress affects our bodies.
- Practice stress-reducing strategies.
- Introduce stress survival toolkit.

Supplies Needed

- Composition notebook for each student in the class
- Level Specific: children's book or video about stress
- Large paper with body outline
- Glue/Glue sticks
- Dry erase board or large paper (optional)
- Body outline worksheets

Introduction

- Level Specific: Icebreaker.

Large Group Instruction/Discussion

- School counselor will ask students to define stress. This can be a verbal discussion, written on a dry erase board or large paper. If written, school counselor can write the word "stress" in the middle of the board/paper and write students' definitions around it.
- School counselor will define good stress versus bad stress. This can be a verbal discussion, written on a dry erase board or large paper. If written, school counselor can create two columns and list examples in each.
- School counselor will display a body outline chart. School counselor will ask students how stress affects their bodies. The body outline chart will be filled in to reflect student answers.

Large Group Activity

- School counselor will teach students the following stress reducing strategies: deep breathing, desk yoga and progressive muscle relaxation.

– Each student will receive an individual composition notebook. They will write their name on their notebook and decorate as time allows.
– School counselor will explain what a stress survival toolkit is and how they will use it.

Small Group/Independent Activity

– Students will complete a body outline worksheet to define where they feel stress in their bodies.
– Students will glue their body outline worksheet into their toolkit.
– As time allows, students may individually practice deep breathing, desk yoga and progressive muscle relaxation.

Closing/Wrap Up

– School counselor will restate what stress is and how students experience it differently in their bodies.
– School counselor will ask students to try using the stress reducing strategies they learned in lesson when they are feeling stressed in school.

Lesson Two

Title of Lesson

How to De-Stress Our Minds

Objective

– Define stress (as learned in lesson one).
– Explain how our minds can increase and decrease stress levels.
– Discuss negative thinking and how it increases stress.
– Explain negative thought stopping.
– Practice stress reducing strategies.

Supplies Needed

– Relaxing music
– Level Specific: trigger trackers
– Stress survival toolkits
– Glue/Glue sticks

Introduction

– Refresher from lesson one: define stress, how we feel it in our bodies, stress reducing strategies.

- School counselor will ask who practiced strategies learned in lesson one.

Large Group Instruction/Discussion

- School counselor will explain how our minds and thoughts can increase stress levels.
- School counselor will ask students to define negative thinking. This can be a verbal discussion, written on a dry erase board or large paper. If written, school counselor can write the words "negative thinking" in the middle of the board/paper and write students' definitions around it.
- School counselor will explain negative thought stopping and how it can be used to lower stress levels.

Large Group Activity

- School counselor will teach students the following stress reducing strategies: positive self-talk, affirmations, cognitive distraction, journaling, meditation, imagery, printables and trigger trackers.
- Each student will receive their stress survival toolkit.
- School counselor will remind them how they will use it.

Small Group/Independent Activity

- Students will complete a trigger tracker worksheet to define when they are feeling stressed.
- Students will glue their trigger tracker worksheet into their toolkit.
- As time allows, students may individually practice positive self-talk, affirmations, cognitive distraction, journaling, meditation and imagery.

Closing/Wrap Up

- School counselor will restate how students experience negative thinking when stressed and how they can use negative thought stopping to decrease their stress.
- School counselor will ask students to try using the stress reducing strategies they learned in lesson when they are feeling stressed in school.

Lesson Three

Title of Lesson

How to Create a Stress Survival Toolkit

Objective

- Go through all stress reducing strategies.
- Complete stress survival toolkits.

Supplies Needed

- Stress survival toolkits
- Level Specific: printables
- Dry erase board or large paper
- Glue/Glue sticks

Introduction

- Refresher from lesson two: negative thinking, negative thought stopping, stress reducing strategies.
- School counselor will ask who practiced using the strategies learned in lesson two.

Large Group Instruction/Discussion

- School counselor will reiterate what stress is, the difference between good and bad stress, how we feel stress in bodies, how we experience negative thinking when stressed.
- School counselor will list stress reducing strategies on large paper.

Large Group Activity

- Students will work to individualize their stress survival toolkits.
- Students will place strategies into their toolkits that are effective in reducing their stress levels.
- Students will glue in printables (Level Specific) that are useful to them in reducing their stress levels.

Small Group Activity

- Students will break into small groups to "show and tell" their stress survival toolkits to classmates and/or the teacher.

Closing/Wrap Up

- School counselor will emphasize that stress is normal and that everyone has it.
- School counselor will ask students how they will use their stress survival toolkits.

– School counselor will remind students to use their stress survival toolkits when needed.

After the conclusion of the last counseling classroom lesson, the school counselor should follow up with students and their teachers. They can complete check ins every few weeks to ask students about their stress levels and see if they are using their stress survival toolkits. A collaboration with teachers both before and after the counseling classroom lessons will help prevent potential discipline concerns related to student's use of their stress survival toolkit. Students should not be fearful of using their toolkits in their classes for fear of getting in trouble with the teacher.

The above lesson template has room for variation as needed. School counselors may also choose to incorporate pre- and posttests to determine the efficacy of the counseling classroom lesson and student stress levels. Counseling classroom lessons about stress can be varied in many different ways to meet the specific needs of the students in the school. There is no one right way for a school counselor to facilitate counseling classroom lessons about student stress.

Conclusion

Every student at any age level can benefit from learning strategies to reduce their stress and/or anxiety. It is important to note not every student has anxiety, nor should they be treated as though they are diagnosed with it. School counselors have the critical job of teaching students what stress and anxiety are, and what they are not. This can be accomplished in individual counseling with students, small counseling groups and counseling classroom lessons.

It is essential the school counselor has a positive and collaborative working relationship with teachers so they understand the levels of anxiety and stress in their students. Teachers will typically be more accepting of the school counselor's time in the classroom or taking students from class when they understand the seriousness of the topic. School counselors can determine the needs of their students and resources available to them. In addition to the tools and strategies discussed, there are an assortment of resources available to school counselors as they plan curricula for anxiety small groups and school counseling classroom lessons for dealing with stress. When used effectively, small counseling groups and counseling classroom lessons for anxiety can be highly useful for students.

The anxiety group was scary, but it was good. None of us really wanted to talk at first. I think we were all terrified to admit anything out loud. But then this one boy started talking about his anxiety. My mouth dropped open because it was like he was saying exactly what was in my brain! We all started talking at the same time after that and the school counselor had to make sure we were taking turns sharing. The way I feel with my anxiety isn't exactly like the other students, but we still had a lot of the same feelings and thoughts. It really made me feel better to know that there are real kids like me right here in my school who have anxiety, too. I'm not happy to know that they have anxiety, but I'm happy that I'm not alone with this.

– Anxious Annie

9 Anxiety Survival Toolkit Use for Classroom Teachers and School Administrators

So I still have anxiety, but I'm learning ways to cope with it. I don't think I'll ever be completely over my anxiety and fears, but there are techniques that help me handle it when I feel like I'm spiraling out of control. My school counselor asked my teacher if she could teach my whole class some ways to deal with stress and anxiety. I hope it will help me and some of the other students in my class who have anxiety. She is also making some anxiety survival toolkits for every classroom in the school! I'm definitely not the only one with anxiety here!

Introduction

School counselors are not the only adults who can provide support to students in dealing with their anxiety. There are other people in the school building who can assist and encourage any age students—teachers, administrators, cafeteria workers, custodians, librarians, school nurses, support staff and bus drivers. Anxiety can influence any number of areas in a student's life. It does not necessarily present itself in an obvious way so all adults understand what the student is experiencing. Some anxious students, regardless of age, may just appear to be quiet or disengaged while struggling internally (Hurley, n.d.). Other students with anxiety may feel as if their brains are useless and engage in inappropriate behaviors to avoid anxiety evoking situations. Every adult who has contact with students should have a basic working knowledge of how to support students with anxiety.

Sometimes anxiety is easy for teachers and other adults in the building to identify. Other times, it can be mistaken for misbehavior, a lack of concern, or defiance. For a student with anxiety, hearing the words "calm down" or "toughen up" from an adult can be devastating (McKibben, 2017). No adult should assume an anxious student has the skill set to calm down or the strength to manage their emotions. School counselors should provide professional development for all school staff to aid them in understanding what anxiety is, what it looks like and how they can assist anxious students. Additionally, school counselors should provide staff an overview of common types of anxieties students may experience, so they will have a better understanding of anxious students. It is crucial for all adults in the building to have a working knowledge about anxiety in order to ensure students are surrounded by a positive support system. This schoolwide support is an important part of assisting students learning to manage their anxiety.

Classroom Use

Classroom teachers can provide varying levels of support based on their students' needs. The more knowledge teachers have about how anxiety impacts their students, the better it will be for students. While a teacher may assume a student is misbehaving, they need to look beyond the misbehavior and consider if the behavior is due to anxiety. Teachers with a working knowledge of anxiety will be more aware of what their students are going through. They will also be prepared to provide interventions to combat their students' anxiety (Morin, n.d.). Additionally, when the classroom teacher works in collaboration with the school counselor, the anxious student will benefit from a strengthened support system. Instead of working at odds with each other, the counselor and teacher will be united and work collaboratively to support the student. In a classroom with two or more students with anxiety, it may be helpful for the teacher to work with the school counselor to schedule counseling classroom lessons involving stress reduction. For anxious students who have worked individually with the school counselor to create an anxiety survival toolkit, the classroom teacher can ensure the student understands how to use the toolkit appropriately in the classroom. The classroom environment can also serve as a support system for students if teachers are willing to provide interventions for students with anxiety (Ehmke, n.d.). The supports that are provided don't need to change the environment of the entire classroom; teachers can provide individualized adjustments to the classroom based on the needs of the anxious student (Morin, n.d.). The most important tool in helping the anxious student is an open communication between the teacher and the school counselor; their work together can provide a foundation for helping a student to cope with their anxiety.

Classroom Support from Teacher

Classroom teachers design their classrooms to provide the best possible learning environments for their students. Trying to meet the individual needs of each student within the classroom can be challenging. The environment of the classroom can either support or hinder a student's ability to manage their anxiety (Truluck, 2019). As school counselors work with classroom teachers, they can assist them in creating a classroom setting that helps all students engage in learning. The school counselor can also help the teacher use specific tools that will aid students in reducing their anxiety. For example, a teacher may choose to set up a relaxing corner or "chill out zone" in their classroom for students (Kennard, 2018).

In order to provide supportive classroom environments for students with anxiety, classroom teachers can:

–   Begin class with a minute or two of meditation and/or relaxing music to help students settle in with a fresh start to the class (McKibben, 2017). This transition time can help the anxious student prepare for the day ahead and lower their anxiety levels.

–   Provide books in the classroom that include characters with anxiety. This serves two purposes: it can help the student feel better about their anxiety and other students can learn to be more understanding of their classmate. Teachers can find a number of books that include the topics of anxiety, stress and worry. Anxious students can feel less isolated from their classmates when these topics are addressed rather than ignored or avoided.

–   Allow the student to sit with them or near an exit during assemblies, pep rallies, etc. The reassurance of the teacher nearby can help a student handle their anxious feelings when they are sitting in large groups. Likewise, sitting near an exit provides a measure of safety and reassurance to an anxious student. They know they are able to leave the situation if it becomes too overwhelming for them.

–   Create small tasks/activities to keep the student busy during down times. Having too much free time during class may increase a student's anxiety, the small tasks/activities provide the student with a distraction or a small goal to accomplish. When engaged in these, their anxiety is less likely to increase.

–   Be certain the student has a class friend designated to assist them as approved. This student can help catch them up when they miss school, which may help the student feel less anxious about returning. The assistance from a designated peer may also feel less distressing than having to ask other classmates for help. The teacher has final approval of the pairing.

–   Provide preferential seating where the student is the most comfortable. This may be close to the door or further away from students who are distracting or disruptive. Students with noticeable behaviors may prefer to sit in the back of the classroom so they don't feel as though they are being watched by their classmates.

–   Determine a signal to use when preparing to call on the student in class. Additionally, allow the student to have another signal to opt out of answering in front of the class. Some anxious students will freeze up and can't respond when unexpectedly called on, even if they know the answer (Ehmke, n.d.).

–   Allow the student the option of typing their answers to tests and/or essays instead of hand writing them. This can be especially helpful for

an anxious student who repeatedly erases and rewrites their answers to the point of distraction. Typing relieves the anxiety that comes with having perfect handwriting or having to rework a problem on paper.
– Allow extended time for tests. Anxious students may get stuck on one question and not be able to move on until they have successfully completed the question. They may also need additional time to express their thoughts on extended answers/essays if they struggle with writing. This may not work for standardized tests that are timed.
– Take breaks for a minute or two to allow students to move around the classroom (Nelson, 2019). This strategy can lower anxiety/stress levels for all students in the classroom. It can also serve to get students refocused on the task at hand. For the anxious student, it may give them the opportunity to release some of their nervous energy and/or distract their minds from their anxiety.
– Help the student readjust when returning to school after being absent. Knowing there is a pile of schoolwork waiting to be made up can increase a student's anxiety. The teacher can modify how the work is to be completed, such as exempting some homework/assignments. It is also helpful for the teacher to provide a time frame for make up work completion. This plan provides structure and allows the anxious student to feel more in control of the situation.
– Modify their expectations when the student is experiencing an especially anxious period. If an anxious student is having a panic attack, the teacher can let the student take a break before starting the next task. The student may respond to their anxiety with undesirable behaviors; teachers should maintain their understanding of anxiety and how it impacts behavior.
– Let the student present projects/reports individually with the teacher instead in front of the entire class. The teacher can also allow the student to videotape their presentation at home and play it for the teacher rather than presenting in person. This allows the student to provide their knowledge of the subject without penalizing them for their anxiety.
– Provide the student with advance notice and reminders of upcoming assessments. Anxious students can be terrified of a pop quiz. Likewise, not knowing a test is coming can also intensify a student's anxiety. Teachers need to consider the type and level of anxiety the student has before using this strategy. For some students with test anxiety, the reminders may incrementally increase their anxiety and fear of taking the test.
– Minimize choices to prevent the student from becoming overwhelmed. Having to make decisions can increase anxiety levels. They can become consumed with what will happen if they make the wrong choice. Teachers can give anxious students a limited number of choices or limit their choices to either/or options.

Emotional Support from Teacher

Emotional support can be just as important as the supportive classroom environment for anxious students. The more knowledge classroom teachers have about anxiety and how to help students, the more likely they are to serve as a positive support system for anxious students. The old saying "students don't care how much you know until they know how much you care" is very poignant for students with anxiety. Their fears are very real to them, and they need to know they will be supported by their teachers as they try to work through their fears. If the classroom teacher doesn't allow the student an opportunity to appropriately manage their anxiety, the student may shut down completely. Learning will be the last thing on their mind. However, if the teacher provides support to the student, that student will likely work even harder to stay in class and learn despite their anxiety (Child Mind Institute, 2016.).

In order to provide emotional support for students with anxiety, classroom teachers can:

- Allow the student to keep their anxiety survival toolkit with them and use it as needed. The student should have been taught how to use their toolkit appropriately by the school counselor; it should not interfere with their learning. While it may seem the student is distracted when using it, they are actually using it to regain control of their anxiety and refocus on their learning. Allowing the student to keep their toolkit with them at their desk provides them with the opportunity to discreetly use it.
- Encourage the student to use their anxiety survival toolkit when they observe the student's anxiety increasing (Morin, n.d.). Teachers can work with the anxious student to come up with a signal or code word the teacher will use when the student starts to exhibit anxious behaviors. This signal or code word reminds the student to get out their toolkit and start using their anxiety reducing strategies.
- Work with the student and school counselor to establish a designated staff member they can visit when they are feeling anxious. This person should be trained and knowledgeable about how to assist with anxiety when a student is sent to them. It doesn't have to be the school counselor—the student may already have a positive, established relationship with another staff member. However, if the student is in crisis, they should see the school counselor.
- Allow the student to call their parent/guardian as a stressful situation arises for additional emotional support. The purpose of this is not to allow the student an opportunity to ask their parents to go home. Sometimes a parent/guardian can provide emotional support an anxious student needs better than anyone else in their lives. Calling the parent also engages them in helping their child positively cope

with their anxiety. A phone call of this type provides a gentle, but firm, reminder that all adults are working to support the student. It also reinforces that the student cannot call the parent and request to go home due to their anxiety.

- Ask the student how they prefer to receive praise (quietly, openly, in writing, with a tangible reward). Specific types of praise may increase anxiety levels for some students, so it is important that the teacher checks with the student to determine which method makes them the least anxious. The answer may be different for different students.
- Engage one on one with a student who is anxious in social situations. Group work can be a trigger for some students as they are afraid of making a mistake and being judged by their classmates. Teachers can strategically group anxious students with those students who are most supportive and understanding of their classmate.
- Be aware of what triggers the student's anxieties. Teachers need to know what types of activities increase the student's anxiety levels. This can happen through a conversation with the student and/or school counselor where the student can share what increases their anxiety in the classroom. The teacher can then engage in preventative measures to reduce the student's anxiety.
- Provide the student an opportunity to take small breaks as needed, such as going to the water fountain or taking a walk down the hall. The teacher may provide a small task for the student, such as taking a note to the front office, in order to discreetly give them an opportunity to take a break when feeling anxious. Some students may prefer to have a card on their desk or a small sticker or token they place in view of the teacher when they are feeling anxious and need a break.
- Allow the student to be paired with friends or a trusted staff member on field trips. This can make the trip more bearable and less anxiety inducing for them. Knowing they have a friend to help them incorporate anxiety reducing strategies goes a long way for an anxious student. If a student is especially anxious, they should be paired with an adult rather than a classmate. Additionally, it may be advantageous to ask the student's parent to chaperone in order to assist managing the student's anxiety.
- (If feasible) provide the student and parent/guardian with advance notice of changes in classroom routines. If the teacher knows they are going to be absent for several days, they can let the parent/guardian of the anxious student know in advance so that they are prepared. This can decrease their anxiety when the change in their routine takes place.
- Validate the student's feelings. An anxious student needs to know the teacher understands them, even when they are not behaving in the most appropriate way. And while the teacher may not agree with their behaviors, the teacher can validate them in order to let the student know they are taking their anxiety seriously.

- Maintain normal boundaries and be consistent with discipline. Although an anxious student is not intentionally trying to get in trouble, letting them get away with breaking the rules does not help them. Neither does providing inconsistent boundaries. Teachers will need to apply the school rules to everyone, including anxious students.
- Encourage independence. Many anxious students don't believe they have the ability to handle everyday challenges, they assume they will fail at tasks. Teachers can help by asking students to complete small tasks and/or errands, such as taking a book to the library or writing the day's agenda on the board. Teachers can also allow anxious students to work to their strengths. For example, they can use flexibility in assigning work to the student by allowing them to complete an assignment in a way they feel comfortable – using technology, making a poster, etc.
- Remind students that mistakes are ok. Perfectionism can be a common symptom of students' anxiety. The prospect of making a mistake is oftentimes more anxiety provoking than the mistake itself. Teachers can remind the anxious student that the student's effort is just as important than getting the answer right.
- Remember not to punish the student for failing to progress or making mistakes. Students don't always use appropriate strategies for handling their anxiety, they may break classroom rules. Teachers need to remember the anxious student is not willfully disobeying them. If the student is working slowly due to their anxiety, the teacher should not punish them for not completing the assignment on time. Additionally, if they make mistakes, they are not doing so on purpose and teachers should not punish them.
- Check in with the student routinely during class. The teacher should make it a point to provide positive interactions with the student each day during class. For example, the teacher can greet an anxious student as they enter the classroom and let them know that they will check in with them in X number of minutes (it might be helpful for the teacher to set an alarm for themselves as a reminder). Once the teacher checks in with the anxious student, they will repeat the process and let the student know that in X number of minutes they will check back in again. When the anxious student knows the teacher will be back, they maintain better self-control.
- Respond to the student with caring and firmness. Anxious students may need constant reassurance that what they are doing is correct. The student may ask a lot of repetitive questions because they are feeling anxious. The teacher can answer the question and let the student know they will only answer questions one time so the student doesn't keep asking their question repeatedly.
- Allow the student to break their work into smaller chunks (Nelson, 2019). When an anxious student sees a 10 page test or 24 math problems for homework, it can overwhelm them and cause them to shut down. The teacher can hand the test out one page at a time or

list six problems on a page. This will allow the student to focus on their work instead of feeling anxious and defeated.

- Model appropriate reactions to stressful situations. Anxious students will benefit from knowing adults get stressed as well. For example, the teacher can have students participate in some deep breathing exercises with them when things are getting hectic in the classroom (McCormac, 2016). This allows the anxious student to feel like they aren't alone in feeling stressed and anxious.
- Ask the student when they normally experience anxiety and about which strategies are most helpful in decreasing their anxiety. Teachers shouldn't assume what is causing a student's anxiety. By asking the student, they will be able to share specific times that are most anxiety producing. The teacher can also learn which strategies from the student's anxiety survival toolkit are most effective for them. When one of those specific times occurs, the teacher will be able to support the anxious student more effectively.

Schoolwide Use

School Support

With the number of students experiencing anxiety rising, it is vital for schools to establish a system of support for anxious students. School counselors can work with administrators and staff to create a school environment that removes as many barriers to student success as possible; this includes emotional barriers as well as academic ones. Schoolwide initiatives, such as anxiety survival toolkits in every classroom, can assist in promoting student success. One of the most imperative tasks the school can take on is to create an atmosphere of caring and calm for all students. Further, a tone of acceptance of all students, regardless of any differences, will help anxious students to be better accepted by their peers.

In order to provide schoolwide systems of support, schools can:

- Start the school year with a stress reducing program for students and staff. This will allow all students to recognize their stressors and learn coping strategies. Anxious students may struggle with the challenge of moving into a different routine and set of rules after a long break. The program can serve as a preventative measure in helping students learn to manage their stress before it becomes problematic.
- Consider lengthening the time between classes so students don't feel so rushed. School in general can produce high levels of stress for students. An anxious student can feel overwhelmed by transitions between classes. If feasible, schools can provide a little extra time between classes so students can experience a quick moment of downtime before their next class.

– Integrate a mental wellness day/week for all students. Every school can benefit from hosting a mental wellness day/week that includes activities that are part of the anxiety survival toolkit. School counselors can lead the activities and all students in the school can participate. This allows all students to have an opportunity to learn and utilize stress-reducing strategies (McCormac, 2016).

– Designate safe places in the building for students when they are feeling very anxious, such as the school counselor's or nurse's office. The administration can designate specific places where the students may go and where an adult will be present.

– Adapt school presentations/plays to include role plays of appropriate coping strategies for anxiety. As any student can benefit from learning positive strategies for lowering stress levels, schools should incorporate positive strategies into the characters/presentation for students to observe. Additionally, it normalizes strategies that anxious students may be using to reduce their anxiety levels.

– Create a lunch buddy program that allows anxious students to eat with a friend. Some anxious students are afraid they will be judged negatively by their peers, so they shy away from sitting with others at lunch. Isolation may temporarily help their anxiety levels, but it is not a long-term solution. Teachers can identify students who may have similar interests to anxious students and allow them to sit together.

– Maintain normal boundaries and be consistent with discipline. While students with anxiety need certain interventions to help them succeed in school, they are not exempt from following school rules or receiving disciplinary actions. Teachers who are educated on what anxiety is and how to help students will be able to determine the differences between anxious misbehavior and regular misbehavior. Further, teachers need to maintain appropriate boundaries with anxious students so they do not receive unfair advantages over other students. Students should not be allowed to use their anxiety as a means for taking advantage of any situation.

– Allow students to opt out of schoolwide assemblies or pep rallies. For some anxious students, all of the excitement and noise at a pep rally can be overwhelming and anxiety producing. The chaotic atmosphere and large crowd can lead to panic attacks. Teachers can let students opt out and go to an alternate location such as the front office or library with a trusted adult.

– Have students come up with positive self-talk statements and post them around the school. This activity can benefit all students, not just those with anxiety. Teachers can partner with school counselors to teach students positive self-talk and how to use it. Once students decide on which positive statements are most meaningful to them, they can write them on posters, butcher paper etc., and post them around the school. This can serve as reminders to students for when they need a positive boost.

- Create a de-stress program for all students immediately before standardized testing starts. Many students, including those without an anxiety disorder, are stressed and anxious when spring testing approaches. A schoolwide program for test de-stressing implemented a week before testing can have a positive impact on anxiety levels for students. The morning of testing, allow students to take five to ten minutes to write out their fears and worries in order to get it out of their systems.
- Make certain the schoolwide calendar isn't overcrowded with activities throughout the school year. Administrators can go through the school's calendar for the entire year to look at how often students have downtime during the year. If they have schoolwide events back to back, they may instead consider creating a break between the events so anxious students aren't overwhelmed.

Adult Support

Although school counselors are specifically trained to work with students with anxiety, any adult in the building can serve as a positive support for students. It is crucial that schools train adults to have a general working knowledge of what anxiety is and how to recognize the warning signs of an anxious student. This training should include all adults in the building, including teachers, administrators, school nurses, office staff, custodial staff, cafeteria workers, hall monitors, school safety/resource officers, teaching assistants, librarians, coaches, bus drivers, administrative assistants and any other certified and support staff in the building. The training does not need to be intense and lengthy. However, school counselors should provide essential information to staff about symptoms and signs of anxiety in students. They should also learn what they should do when engaging with an anxious student. In addition, staff need to know what to do if they encounter a student in crisis. After this training, if a staff member observes a student experiencing a panic attack or behaving in a particular manner, they will have the tools to appropriately interact with and assist the student in decreasing their anxiety. They will also have a better understanding of what to do if they come across an anxious student who is in crisis.

In order to provide a positive support system for students, adults in the school building can:

- Learn about different anxiety disorders as well as the symptoms of each. Adults in the building will not be diagnosing students with anxiety, but need a general understanding of symptoms or behaviors an anxious student might exhibit. If they encounter a student experiencing anxiety, the adult will be equipped to help them.

- Encourage students to balance their academic demands so they don't become overwhelmed with too many challenging classes. Many anxious students put academic pressure on themselves when choosing their course loads for the year. If they don't sign up for the most challenging courses they may feel like they aren't smart or capable of succeeding. Adults in the school can make certain the anxious student doesn't overload their courses and therefore increase their anxiety levels.
- Ask students which interventions are most helpful in decreasing their anxiety. Adults in the school shouldn't assume which interventions are helpful in reducing a student's anxiety. By talking to the student, they will be able to share what is causing their anxiety. The adult can then ask the student which strategies are most helpful in lowering their anxiety levels.
- School counselors and administrators should work with families to create an attendance plan that works with the anxious student rather than against them. Discuss attendance options for the student, such as a shortened school day or a reward system for the student when they come to school. While it's not ideal for any student to miss school, the longer a student with anxiety avoids coming to school the more challenging it is for them to return. When the student is at school, they can work on utilizing their anxiety survival toolkit and work to have a set of strategies in place to help them stay in school the entire day. The plan will depend on the needs of the student.
- Ask the student how they prefer to receive praise (quietly, openly, in writing, with a tangible reward). Specific types of praise may increase anxiety levels for some students, so it is important the teacher checks with the student to determine which method makes them the least anxious. The answer may be different for different students.
- Respond to students with caring and firmness. Students feel they are alone with their anxiety. Knowing that an adult in the building cares about their well-being can go a long way for an anxious student. However, it is important for the adult to maintain a firm demeanor with the student so that the student does not exploit the adult's concern for them.
- Encourage independence. Many anxious students don't believe they have the ability to handle everyday challenges, they assume they will fail at tasks. Adults in the building can provide the student with small tasks in order to boost the student's sense of independence. They may need to start with very small tasks in order to build the student's self-confidence. The adult can then allow the anxious student to work more on tasks more independently.
- Remind students that mistakes are ok. Perfectionism is a common symptom of student anxiety. The prospect of making a mistake is oftentimes more anxiety provoking than the mistake itself.

Adults in the building can remind the anxious student that their mistakes are part of learning and then engage them in anxiety-reducing strategies.

- Modify expectations when the student is experiencing an especially anxious period. Adults in the school may allow anxious students to use strategies to alleviate their anxiety. For example, an administrator may allow a student who is experiencing high levels of anxiety to leave class a few minutes early to avoid crowded hallways.

- Keep a positive attitude about students' anxieties. Adults at school might find it difficult at times to maintain a positive attitude toward a student with anxiety. Their behaviors can be challenging for the adult to permit at school, so the adult needs to take a step back and remember what is going on behind the anxious student's behavior.

- Model appropriate reactions to stressful situations. Although the hope is that a schoolwide crisis never occurs, stressful situations do occur. Some examples are power outages and fire drills. These occasional situations can be mildly stressful for most students; but a student with anxiety may find these to be especially anxiety producing. Adults in the building can help all students by remaining calm and reminding themselves in front of students to follow protocols. This can alleviate some of the anxiety the student is feeling.

Conclusion

Students with anxiety disorders don't always ask for help. Therefore, it is imperative adults in the school setting know and understand what anxiety is and how that differs from normal stress. They don't diagnose students, but they need to recognize the red flags related to anxiety. A common vocabulary around the school regarding anxiety is vital to successfully assisting anxious students. School counselors need to establish positive working relationships with teachers and other adults in the building in order to develop and implement appropriate systems for students with anxiety.

Teachers can work to increase their awareness of anxiety and how to accommodate it in their classrooms. They first need to consider the environment in their classrooms—how they set the mood for students from the moment they walk in until the moment they leave. Teachers should consider what tools they put into place in their classroom, such as calming music, books that include characters with anxiety, corners or an area in the class for anxious students to lower their anxiety levels, seating arrangements and small breaks for students. These small changes in the classroom can provide a great deal of support for a student with anxiety.

In addition to the classroom environment, the teacher's understanding can serve as a meaningful support for an anxious student. This support can come through the ways they provide accommodations to the anxious student's learning. Emotionally supporting the student may be viewed by the anxious student as equally important, if not more important to them. When an anxious student feels as though the teacher is sincerely trying to understand and help them with their anxiety, they are more likely to work harder to control their anxiety. A teacher who encourages the use of their anxiety survival guide in the class provides the student with a positive support system in the classroom.

Entire schools can institute schoolwide strategies and programs to help anxious students. This should happen throughout the entire school setting and should be incorporated from the top down. When the administration supports mental wellness days/weeks and provides destressing programs for students, it sets the expectation for how staff in the building should regard the seriousness of the topic. How the adults respond to anxiety in the school will set the tone for how students react to it. Schools can work to support their anxious students by providing quiet, safe spaces. within the school, allowing them to sit out of pep rallies and/or assemblies, creating lunch buddy programs, and providing consistency with their rules. Students flourish when the rules are consistent, so enforcing them with a caring attitude will help anxious students to understand their boundaries.

All adults in the school building are responsible for the academic success of the students inside. School counselors, teachers and administrators are not the only adults in the school who are responsible for the emotional well-being of students. All adults in the school building are capable of providing emotional support to anxious students. Training will serve the purpose of assisting adults in the building to understand what anxiety is and how to support anxious students. While training is essential, it does not take a degree in school counseling to care about and positively engage with anxious students. Adults need to maintain firm and consistent boundaries along with appropriate disciplinary measures as needed, but their support and encouragement of anxious students can help those students to find more success at school.

Although all of these tools may not be feasible to implement in classrooms and/or schoolwide, schools play a vital role in the academic and emotional success of students. Depending on the school and classroom setting, adjustments may have to be made to the different supports provided to anxious students. However, many of the tools described in this chapter are easily implementable because they require adults in the school to care about an anxious student's emotional and academic success. School counselors can lead the school in its journey to create an atmosphere of acceptance and support for students with anxiety. Administrators can support and endorse the efforts of the school counselor, which leads to more buy-in from all adults in the school building. When everyone in the school supports an anxious student, that student has a much higher chance of experiencing success in dealing with their anxiety.

My teacher got out the anxiety survival toolkit for our classroom today when we finished work for the day. She explained what it was and how we can use it in the class. She knows that I have anxiety but she made sure the other students in my class don't know. We got to go through some of the different techniques that students can use to help them when they are stressed or anxious. The teacher put us in small groups to practice the strategies. I was really nervous with my small group, because I felt like they were going to be able to instantly tell that I have anxiety. No one seemed to notice anything. They even complimented me on how good of a job I did on the meditation activities!

– Anxious Annie

10 Positive Outlook for Students with Anxiety

Some days are better than others. I feel like I'm getting a grip on my anxiety instead of it having a grip on me. I have to remember there are people around who can help me when I'm going through a tough time and my anxiety gets unbearable. There is just still so much that I have to learn in order to figure out how I'm going to live the rest of my life knowing I have anxiety. The rest of this school year feels more achievable, although I do get scared thinking about next school year and the next school year and the next school year. I don't go straight into a panic when I think about what life will be like when I'm an adult, but it is scary to think about it.

– Anxious Annie

Introduction

Stress is something everyone deals with at different times in their lives. However, anxiety is a serious epidemic among children and teenagers. This epidemic is also prevalent among many adults who struggle through their everyday lives. Anxiety can negatively impact students' learning and lead to other emotional difficulties if not treated. If students do not receive help for their anxiety, they will live in fear and rob themselves of the opportunity to experience rich and meaningful lives. They will not feel the freedom of living a healthy lifestyle, the control in making their own choices, a sense of belonging with others or the ability to have the fun they want in their lives. Anxiety is not something to defeat; it will exist on some level in every student's life. There will be setbacks from time to time, which is a normal part of life.

Anxiety is also much more common than students realize. When they work with their school counselor to understand their anxiety, they can take steps to manage it and gain control of their lives.

Students will react differently toward different strategies intended to help reduce their anxiety. Some types of anxieties students experience will respond well to the strategies detailed in this book. The anxiety survival toolkit they create can grow and change with them as they mature. Other students may need more intensive interventions in addition to their anxiety survival toolkit, including therapy and/or medication. Research on anxiety (Anxiety and Depression Association of America, n.d., Facts and Statistics) overwhelmingly suggests a combination of therapy and medication provides the most long-term success for individuals with anxiety. Be that as it may, not every student has access to therapy and/or medication to help with their anxiety. In addition to lack of access, not all parents support the use of medication in treating emotional issues. This is where the student's anxiety survival toolkit can prove extremely useful both in and out of the school setting. While the toolkit does not replace medication and/or therapy, it does provide the student with an individualized, tangible and effective set of strategies to use as they learn to cope with their anxiety. As students use the five whys to determine why they experience anxiety, they can begin to actively work toward reducing their anxiety. They can then see and feel a positive change in their emotional well-being when they utilize their toolkits.

A school counselor's job does not end with the creation of the anxiety survival toolkit. They need to confirm that the student thoroughly understands how and when to use it. The school counselor also needs to verify other adults in the school are both aware and supportive of the student using their toolkit. This begins with training all school staff in understanding what anxiety is and how they can help students in need. It continues with designating common vocabulary for the school to use when working with students with anxiety. More specifically, school counselors should create a collaborative working relationship with teachers to support students (Edwards & Cadenhead, 2009). Teachers should understand why and how an anxious student will use their anxiety survival toolkit in the classroom. As teachers work with school counselors, they will learn how to create a supportive classroom environment for anxious students and have tools for emotionally supporting those students as well.

In addition to working individually with students to create their anxiety survival toolkit, school counselors can work with anxious students in small counseling groups to create their toolkits. The school counselor can also teach strategies for reducing anxiety and stress to entire classrooms of students. Further, they can work with the administration to implement mental wellness days/weeks into the school year for the entire student population. All students can participate in learning positive ways to deal with their stress and/or anxiety. Each classroom can benefit from having its own relaxation/de-stress kit for student use. In utilizing these different methods for working with students and staff in the school, school counselors can aid anxious students in learning the benefits of creating an anxiety survival toolkit.

Support Systems

Many students tend to feel alone in their anxiety. Their ages and grade levels do not increase or decrease this perception. For a number of younger students, they may not yet understand they even have anxiety.

Therefore, they don't understand how to describe what they are feeling to others. Students at the middle/junior high school level may not always be able to distinguish their thoughts and feelings between those of adolescence and puberty and those of anxiety. Anxious high school students may feel detached from their peers and feel that no one else understands what they are going through. All of these can create a sense of isolation in students trying to regulate their anxiety. However, students experiencing anxiety should not suppress their anxious feelings or avoid seeking help from others. In today's society, students are never alone. There are vast networks of support systems available to students of all ages that are eager to assist students coping with anxiety (National Alliance of Mental Illness, 2017). Knowing who they can count on in their lives is key to helping anxious students build their support systems (The American Institute of Stress, 2019). There are resources both in person and electronically that anxious students can use to help themselves.

When considering electronic resources, caution should be used due to the uncertain nature of content on the internet. Even though some anxious students can gain access to online resources by simply looking up the word "anxiety" on their phones, they should consult with a trusted adult before utilizing any resources. School counselors should be available to provide anxious students with age-appropriate online resources if the student would like to use them. Students should also understand that although they can use online resources to help with their anxiety, they do not serve as a replacement for human interactions and the live resources available to them. Many of students' sources of anxiety come from their interactions with others and real-life situations, so an electronic support will not be able to provide all the support needed to manage their anxiety.

An appropriate website can provide ideas for dealing with anxiety, but the student will need to physically try out the idea in their real life in order to gauge its usefulness. A number of valuable online resources are available to students. There are websites that provide clear and accurate information about what anxiety is and how it is diagnosed, such as:

- https://adaa.org/ (Anxiety and Depression Association of America)
- https://www.nami.org/learn-more/mental-health-conditions/anxiety-disorders (National Alliance of Mental Illness)
- https://www.nimh.nih.gov/health/topics/anxiety-disorders/index.shtml (National Institute of Mental Health)

There are numerous online support groups for students and adults with anxiety. Again, these websites are not appropriate for younger students in elementary or middle/junior high school. Keep in mind some are not even appropriate for high school students. An online anxiety support group can provide particular support for older students, such as the convenience of having someone around to listen 24 hours a day

(Anxiety and Depression Association of America, n.d., Online Support Group).

Anxiety doesn't limit itself to the school day, so a teenager experiencing anxiety at home may benefit from the use of an online support group. An online support group can also provide a teenager the comfort and safety of anonymity where they can receive support from others with anxiety. However, caution should be used when researching appropriate online support systems. While many are intended to provide a positive support system to those living with anxiety, there are also sites that perpetuate a lot of the negative thinking associated with anxiety. Miscommunication can occur online, because the student may not always be able to articulately transfer their anxiety into written words. This may lead to frustration and online disagreements, which can increase the student's anxiety. Some anxiety support group members may also provide misinformation regarding anxiety. Group members may be well intentioned and/or see themselves as experts on anxiety, which can be dangerous for a high school student or adult looking for answers. Even though some students don't have access to a medical doctor, online support groups are not a replacement for sound medical advice. If an older student is uncertain about the appropriateness of an anxiety website, they should ask their parent, school counselor and/or another trusted adult to determine whether it is a suitable source of support or not. Appropriate websites for anxiety support groups may include:

- https://www.dailystrength.org/group/anxiety (Daily Strength Anxiety Support Group)
- https://adaa.org/adaa-online-support-group (Anxiety and Depression Association of America Online Support Group)
- https://www.inspire.com/groups/mental-health-america/ (Mental Health America: Mental health support group and discussion community)
- https://www.facebook.com/ many online anxiety support groups such as:
  - Anxiety Lounge
  - Anxiety, Depression and Mental Health Support Group
  - Worry Warrior Anxiety Support Group
  - Anxiety Support Group

Older students and adults with anxiety may prefer both electronic and in person support groups. Both types of groups provide unique benefits that can be utilized by the student. The most valuable tool is one the student will use when they need it. The intention of these websites is not to help a student self-diagnose themselves with anxiety. They are also not a replacement for in person resources students can find within the school setting. They should instead be used as additional support for students who want to learn more.

Numerous support systems are available to anxious students both inside and outside of the school setting (Anxiety and Depression Association of America, n.d., Online Support Groups). Within the school setting, fellow students, school counselors, teachers, administrators, nurses, support staff, cafeteria workers, custodial staff, bus drivers, coaches, school resource officers, librarians and anyone else in the school building are all potential supports for an anxious student. The responsibility to provide a support system for students with anxiety does not rest solely with the school counselor.

Schools have a responsibility to ensure success and provide support for every student. It is vital that the school actively works to build a system of support for students dealing with anxiety. Students should be able to seek out others in the building who will positively support them when they are experiencing anxiety. They need to know who their supports are in school, how to access them and when to access them. Anxious students should work with their school counselors to identify and understand how and when to use their support system at school. The ultimate goal for anxious students is to manage their anxiety on their own – and then use their support systems as needed. Students should not overuse their support systems; they should work toward independence and using their anxiety survival toolkits as a first line of defense against their anxiety.

Negative students and adults should not be part of a student's support system. Some friends of students are not supportive when they are feeling anxious; they can increase the student's anxiety because they dismiss their feelings or don't really listen when the student needs it. Unfortunately, every school will have some teachers and adults unwilling or unable to be supportive on a daily basis. These adults will not serve well as a positive support for anxious students.

Outside the school setting, friends, siblings, parents, grandparents and other extended family members, spiritual leaders, coaches, community group leaders and many other people can provide a network of support for a student with anxiety (Feldman, 2018). Their roles are similar to adults in the school; however, they don't have the limitations that a school imposes. The student can choose which people in their lives provide the best support system and help to lower their anxiety. These people provide a number of supports that create results as those from their anxiety survival toolkit. The goal for these supports is not to eliminate all of the student's anxiety. Although this idea is well intentioned, it can lead to overprotecting the student and creating a negative cycle that exacerbates that student's anxiety. People who care about and love the anxious student want to protect them from their fears. Unfortunately, that keeps the anxious student from feeling empowered to manage their anxiety.

Some helpful pointers for people serving as part of a support system for anxious students both in and out of school include:

–   Don't try to remove all of the stressors in the students' lives. Although excessive anxiety can be debilitating, some anxiety is a normal part of life. Overprotection does not serve any good purpose in allowing a student to grow into a healthy adult (McCormac, 2016). Instead of overprotection, supporters should help the student learn ways to live with their anxiety.

–   Encourage the student to discuss their feelings about their anxiety. When discussing their feelings, it is more helpful to ask open-ended questions, such as "How are you feeling about your upcoming presentation?" rather than leading questions such as "Are you anxious about your presentation? Are you worried it won't go well?" This can lead the student to assume they are supposed to feel anxious, even when they may not.

–   Model healthy ways to cope with anxiety. Everyone is faced with anxiety-provoking situations, so letting the student see how others cope in healthy ways can be empowering to them. Young and older students alike are very perceptive and will observe how other people react when they are faced with an anxious situation. If they see people in their support system reacting with positive strategies, they are more likely to try to embody that strategy themselves.

–   Don't allow one negative situation to reinforce how the student should react every time when faced with that situation. For example, if a student has a panic attack in an elevator, their support system shouldn't say or infer that the student is going to have that reaction again the next time they get on an elevator. They should be careful not to respond in a way that makes the student think they *should* be worried about having another panic attack the next time they ride the elevator.

–   Provide emotional and verbal support without empowering their negative feelings. A person in the student's support system can validate their fears and anxiousness without agreeing with them. This allows the person to support the student without intensifying their anxiety.

–   Don't allow the student to avoid everything that makes them anxious. While it may provide a short-term solution to the student's anxiety, it teaches the wrong coping mechanism (the flight response) for handling anxiety. Then every time the student is presented with something that increases their anxiety, they will cycle into their flight response rather than learning to use their anxiety survival toolkit. An anxiety-provoking situation is the perfect time for someone from the student's support system to help them work through their feelings and use their anxiety-reducing strategies.

- Talk through the student's anxieties with them to come up with a plan to handle themselves if what they are anxious about comes true. For example, if a student is anxious about going to spend the night at a friend's house, the student and their support person can talk through steps the student can take if they are feeling anxious at the friend's house – use strategies from their anxiety survival toolkit, think through what fun, good things can happen at their friend's house, call their parent/guardian for encouragement, etc.
- Help them let go of the past. If they dwell on past events that caused them anxiety, students will not be able to deal with the present moment. Refocus their thoughts and energies toward the current situation in order to deal with what is in front of them.
- Engage in healthy coping strategies for anxiety with the student. Go for walks, exercise, volunteer to help others etc.

Different age groups will respond differently to assistance from people in their support systems. It is reassuring to know they are not alone in their anxiety, no matter their age. Understanding who they can add to their anxiety support system lets the student know they can choose people who bring positivity and encouragement to their lives. They do not need to include people who are negative and/or reinforce their anxiety. Other important factors for successful support systems include knowing how and when students can access people in their support system. Students can build an entire network of support for themselves – at school, at home and potentially online that allow them to positively cope with their anxiety. They need to know who they can count on to help them when they feel their anxiety increasing. There is an empowerment for anxious students in knowing they can not only use their anxiety survival toolkits but also reach out to others who will help them through their anxiety.

Long-Term Management of Anxiety

Anxiety disorders are the most common mental disorders in adults in the United States, with roughly 40 million adults aged 18 and older being affected by it. That is close to 20% of the adult population in the United States affected each year. According to the Anxiety and Depression Association of America, approximately 25% of children aged 13–17 experience issues with anxiety disorders each year; most individuals diagnosed with anxiety see their symptoms develop before the age of 21. Anxiety is not limited to those living in the United States. Around 3.6% of individuals worldwide, about 264 million people, are affected by anxiety according to the World Health Organization. All of the following supports are applicable to both students and adults. For the purposes of this book, however, long-term management will focus on the student's well-being with the understanding that adults may benefit from utilizing the strategies as well.

Students with anxiety often ask their school counselors if there is a cure for their anxiety. They want to stop it altogether. Although there is no official cure for anxiety, there are various ways a student can learn to manage their anxiety (Goldstein, n.d.). In the present, anxiety can feel overwhelming and impossible to handle. However, school counselors can work with anxious students to create their anxiety survival toolkit in order to help them more effectively manage their anxiety. These strategies can be used throughout the rest of their lives so that their anxiety doesn't prohibit them from living as healthy, functioning adults. Anxiety doesn't necessarily get worse as a student grows up and becomes an adult. Different life stressors may present new challenges and fears into a person's life, yet they can still use effective strategies to prevent their anxiety from increasing. However, if a person with anxiety allows themselves to live in constant fear, they will deprive themselves of the opportunity to live a rich and satisfying life. Additionally, if their lifestyle is stressful and unhealthy, they are more likely to experience higher levels of anxiety. Individuals have to make the choice either to create their world with hope and control over their anxiety or to let their anxiety shape and control the world they live in.

Long-term management of anxiety is most successful when a student focuses both on their physical and mental health. Since anxiety can impact all areas of a student's life, it is important for them to focus on ways to manage it during challenging times (Feldman, 2018). Students with anxiety may or may not have access to a doctor, so the use of medication to treat anxiety may be dependent on the availability of medical care. Even with available medical care, many people choose not to use medications to treat a mental disorder for a number of reasons. Additionally, cognitive-behavioral therapy has proven to be a successful intervention for students with anxiety. Access to mental health professionals may be limited for some students. Many parents also choose not to engage their children in therapy for different reasons. Ideally, a partnership of medication and cognitive-behavioral therapy provides the best combination of support for students in successfully treating their anxiety (Mayo Clinic, n.d.). Not every student will be able or willing to receive this combination of treatment for anxiety. It is dependent on a variety of factors, such as availability of services, parental willingness to allow medications for their child, student willingness to take medications, parental willingness and ability to afford cognitive-behavioral therapy for their child and willingness of the student to engage in cognitive-behavioral therapy. As school counselors do not provide therapy of any kind to students, parents will have to seek therapy outside of the school setting. Some parents may be unable or unwilling to find a therapist outside of the school to work with their child's anxiety.

When considering the long-term management of their anxiety, students should strive to live a healthy lifestyle. Physically healthy habits don't eliminate anxiety, but they certainly work to decrease symptoms of anxiety (Mayo Clinic, n.d.). Although students may not be able to control all aspects of their physical health, including financial limitations regarding healthy food purchases, they can work to control their levels of physical activity both in and out of the school. Exercise has been shown to improve some symptoms of anxiety, so when available, students should choose to engage in activities that allow them to be physically active. For example, if a school provides the opportunity for a student to participate in physical education each year, the student should take advantage of it. Further, if the student has the opportunity to participate in a sport activity at a recreational or competitive level, they should strive to do so. For students without access or the ability to participate in sports, physical activities such as yoga and meditation can work to reduce their anxious symptoms. Sleep can also play a role in a student's ability to effectively manage their anxiety. Poor sleeping habits can exacerbate a student's anxiety; a good night's sleep can lessen a student's anxious feelings and thoughts.

A student's diet can also impact their anxiety levels, so in order to manage their anxiety long term, they need to try to eat meals that are healthy and nutritious balanced. Again, some students may not have access to healthy and nutritious foods, so they may try to eat the healthiest food available to them. Some students may have food sensitivities; they should be aware of which foods may cause them irritation that may bring on more anxiety. Caffeine can also play a role in increasing a student's anxiety. Energy drinks and high volumes of coffee or soda can increase anxiety and should be avoided in large doses. Nicotine can play a role in increasing anxiety; it is a powerful stimulant and does not decrease anxiety. Some students attempt to self-medicate through the use of alcohol and/or drugs. In addition to being illegal to students, they can create more of an emotional imbalance in students with anxiety. In the long term, the use of alcohol and/or drugs can disrupt a student's sleep cycles, interfere with other medications and create additional problems in their lives – increasing their anxiety even more.

As students with anxiety focus on the long-term management of their mental health, they should work to learn strategies that they can use in different areas of their lives. School counselors are an integral part of an anxious student's support system at school, so long-term management often begins with them. The creation of an anxiety survival toolkit empowers an anxious student to learn strategies at a young age that they can carry with them throughout the rest of their lives. School counselors can work with students to teach them a number of strategies to use in coping with their anxiety. Although it is not cognitive-behavioral therapy, many of the strategies used by school counselors are intended to help change a student's thought patterns and behaviors. One of the most practical benefits to creating anxiety survival toolkits with school counselors is that it is free. Parents do not have to pay for a school counselor to teach their child strategies for managing their anxiety. Even more beneficial to the student is their ability to use the toolkit in every area of their lives, not just in school. Anxious students can work to become experts on their anxiety, from why they have it, what it is they are trying to achieve and how to handle it. As part of their toolkit, students can build their own personal library of books, websites or support groups that are helpful to them.

When students start to gain a better handle on their anxiety, they can better identify ways to think more in terms of long-term management of it. They can learn what their triggers and stressors are, and when they present in their lives, they can then plan accordingly. For example, if an anxious student has learned that large groups bring on panic attacks, they can make arrangements with the school counselor to sit out of a pep rally. As an adult, they can continue to be mindful of that trigger and plan their days to avoid triggers and stressors that may bring on a panic attack. They may choose to avoid going to the grocery store on Saturdays when it is the most crowded, and instead go on a Monday afternoon when it isn't busy. Knowing their triggers and stressors will enable anxious students to transition into adulthood with a better mindset that will allow them to live with fewer limitations.

Long-term management of anxiety is key to enabling an individual to have a healthy and productive life (Mayo Clinic, n.d.). If left untreated, they may face challenges in trying to get through each day. For example, a student without support systems in place for their anxiety may live every day in a continual state of worry and tension. As an adult, they may struggle to stay employed, maintain relationships or even become too fearful to leave their homes. The strategies learned for coping with their anxiety will come into play as they encounter different stressors in their adult lives. During adulthood, there will be times when individuals may not even be aware of what new situations may trigger their anxiety (The American Institute of Stress, 2019). It is impossible for them to prepare themselves for every single potential situation they may or may not encounter during their lives. There may be times when they experience a panic attack without any warning. However, if individuals have already learned anxiety-reducing strategies in their youth, they will be able to apply them when unexpected situations come up. Most importantly, individuals should make certain they continue to utilize their toolkits throughout their adult lives. If they have been issued medications to assist with their anxiety, they should continue to take them as directed. Numerous people are prescribed medication for their anxiety, but as soon as it starts working some stop taking it. The purpose of medications used to treat anxiety is not to cure it with a short-term prescription. Depending on the severity of their anxiety, individuals need to consistently take their medication with the understanding that they may take them long-term. If a student or adult is in therapy to treat their anxiety, it is important that they keep their appointments and continue therapy as long as needed. Learning about and appropriately treating their anxiety will be crucial to their management of it. There are no short-term solutions to anxiety, nor is there a "cure" for it. However, long-term management is the key that will lead to successful management of anxiety (National Alliance of Mental Illness, 2017). Consistently using their anxiety survival toolkits and resources will allow a student to know there is hope for living a healthy and productive life while successfully managing their anxiety.

Hope for the Future

Friedrich Nietzsche is quoted as saying "the future influences the present as much as the past." A student's views of their anxiety can strongly influence how they choose to manage it. Living with negativity and doubt will only perpetuate and increase their anxiety levels. Dwelling on past anxiety and failures can prevent a student from effectively dealing with the current situation they are in. Likewise, being anxious about the future does not help a student to cope with their anxiety. Unfortunately, anxiety does not limit itself to past, present or future experiences (Ginsburg & Kinsman, 2014). Students may experience anxiety once and then become fearful of what will happen if they experience anxiety again. This ties their anxiety to their past experiences, which in turn creates anxieties about future experiences. The student's present situation is not truly experienced because they are feeling anxious about the past or the future. This cycle of fear can be never ending if the student does not effectively manage their anxiety. It can rob them of valuable experiences because they never get to actually experience them due to being trapped in their negative thought cycle. Without hope that they can manage their anxiety in the present, they will not have hope for their future.

Turning on the news and seeing wars, death, kidnappings, hate and negativity – these toxic stories can perpetuate the negativity that streams through students' lives. It may be difficult for some students to find hope amid a world of suffering and adversity. However, students who choose to live with positivity and hope for the future will more successfully regulate their anxiety (Truluck, 2019). While some people may stigmatize anxiety and those that have it, students can learn to both understand and positively approach their anxiety. An important factor in their success in treating anxiety is reducing the negative stigma around it. Understanding their anxiety and seeking help for it turns them from being fragile and embarrassed into strong and destigmatized students.

Students with anxiety can experience positive feelings of hope and trust when they surround themselves with their support systems. School counselors can serve as a positive support for anxious students by empowering them to choose their attitudes and approach toward their anxiety. Schools can surround their anxious students with hope for their present and their futures. When anxious students learn resilience in managing challenges in their lives, they begin to see a better outlook on what their futures will bring. Anxiety management becomes a constructive part of who they are and how they function on a daily basis. The future stops being seen as a thing to be feared and starts to be seen in a more positive light. Instead of negative relationships, poor coping skills and a lack of hope, anxious students begin to find themselves in positive relationships, using their anxiety survival toolkits and hoping for positive outcomes for their adult lives.

Learning the habit of hope is crucial to the successful treatment of anxiety in students. While they may tend to dwell in the past and present, they must learn to embrace hope for the future in order to have the courage to gain control over their anxiety. Hope is the tool that can work to eliminate fear and increase a student's inner courage. When anxious students begin to hope for their future, they may catch themselves not worrying as much. As they use their toolkits with the hope that their strategies will work, they may find their panic attacks decreasing in length or altogether at times. Hope prevents anxious students from staying lost in their own minds. It brings their minds alive with future aspirations rather than obsessive negative thinking. Hope also allows students to understand that although there is no quick fix for their anxiety, they will still be okay in learning to live with it. They will exercise better follow-through with their strategies because they are motivated and encouraged to pursue positive management of their anxiety.

Although it can be difficult at times, remaining positive and having hope allows anxious students to see better long-term results in reducing their anxiety. Some students are not naturally optimistic, so it may be more challenging for them to use hopeful thinking as a strategy for decreasing their anxiety. Nevertheless, their hope is essential in creating a better future for themselves. It may take some adjustments to their lifestyles and ways of thinking, but hope for the future can bring about better management of their anxious feelings. Having hope can also help students to replace their negative thoughts and support their positive thinking. They can envision a future where they achieve academic success, have meaningful relationships with others, work, participate in activities and successfully regulate their anxiety. With support and their anxiety survival toolkit, anxious students can live with hope for both a well-adjusted childhood and adult life.

Conclusion

Everyone will experience stress at some point in their lives. Almost everyone will also have to confront anxiety about some event that occurs during their childhood and/or adolescence. While many people think that anxiety is a choice and that those with it can decide to stop worrying so much, it is not that simple. No one has ever made the choice to feel anxious or develop an anxiety disorder. A student with anxiety cannot turn it on and off like a light switch, nor do they choose to have it as part of their daily lives. Anxiety can be both distressing and debilitating for students. If there was a switch to turn off anxiety, students would gratefully flip it off and stop struggling to cope with it. Anxiety can affect their ability to learn, engage in friendships, work and participate in life activities. When left untreated, a student with anxiety grows into an adult with anxiety who has difficulty with maintaining employment and relationships with family and friends.

Knowing what anxiety is and what types there are is the key to understanding how to help students who are experiencing it. School counselors should not only educate themselves but also train others in the school setting in order to help the student receive the support they need. Anxious students need to understand why they are feeling anxiety, what basic need they are trying to fulfill and how they are going to go about reducing their anxiety. Their work with the school counselor will include the creation of their individualized anxiety survival toolkit. Students can create the toolkit based on their individual needs and comfort level with different strategies for reducing their anxiety. It is vital that students have a support system consisting of various adults and students that substantially impacts their anxiety levels in positive ways, and school counselors can work with anxious students to determine and utilize their support systems. As anxious students learn to employ their support systems and anxiety survival toolkits, they will find better success in decreasing their anxiety. Throughout their lives, they will need to continue using those strategies to effectively treat their anxiety. While their anxiety will never completely vanish, anxious students should have hope that they can still live happy and productive lives.

Students with anxiety should not be too hard on themselves. At times it will feel overwhelming, but there are many steps they can take to combat it. There will be setbacks – times when they feel like they've beaten their anxiety, only to find that they still have to work at it. They may feel as though they've mastered how to manage their anxiety but will still need to learn new strategies for better management of their anxiety. There is no magic cure for anxiety. Instead of seeing anxiety as their enemy, addressing it head-on with treatment is necessary in order for a student to successfully manage it. Strategies to treat anxiety will be used differently for each student depending on their age, developmental level and type of anxiety. School counselors find that students will experience the best success in managing their anxiety when they use their anxiety survival toolkits to self-regulate their emotions rather than trying to figure out how to make themselves free from any anxiety. Students have the power to navigate themselves into positive outcomes ... although they are not alone one their journey.

There is hope! I am always going to have anxiety. And I understand better now that there is no 'magic cure' to fix my anxiety. I don't want to let all of my fear and anxiety keep me from living my life. I'm going to have days when I don't want to get out of bed; I'm going to have days where I don't feel overwhelmed by my anxiety. I'll have to just take one day at a time. Sometimes, when my anxiety is bad I'll have to take it an hour at a time, or a moment at a time. My parents, my school counselor and my friends are good supports to me. My anxiety is part of who I am, but it is not who I am and it doesn't define me.

References

Allen, N., Capron, D., Lejuez, C., Reynolds, E., Macpherson, L., & Schmidt, N. (2014). Developmental trajectories of anxiety symptoms in early adolescence: The influence of anxiety sensitivity. *Journal of Abnormal Child Psychology*, 42(4), 589–600.

American Academy of Child & Adolescent Psychiatry. (n.d.). *Advances in child and adolescent anxiety disorder research.* Retrieved from https://www.aacap.org/AACAP/Medical_Students_and_Residents/Mentorship_Matters/DevelopMentor/Advances_in_Child_and_Adolescent_Anxiety_Disorder_Research.aspx.

American Academy of Pediatrics. (2017, May 4). *Children's hospitals admissions for suicidal thoughts, actions double during past decade.* Retrieved from https://www.aappublications.org/news/2017/05/04/PASSuicide050417.

American Psychiatric Association. (2013). *Diagnostic and statistical manual of mental disorders* (5th ed.). Arlington, VA.

Anxiety and Depression Association of America. (n.d.). *ADAA online support group.* Retrieved from https://adaa.org/adaa-online-support-group.

Anxiety and Depression Association of America. (n.d.). *Anxiety and depression.* Retrieved from https://adaa.org/sites/default/files/ADAA_Anx&Dep.pdf.

Anxiety and Depression Association of America. (n.d.). *Anxiety disorders in children.* Retrieved from https://adaa.org/sites/default/files/Anxiety%20Disorders%20in%20Children.pdf.

Anxiety and Depression Association of America. (n.d.). *Facts and statistics.* Retrieved from https://adaa.org/about-adaa/press-room/facts-statistics.

Anxiety and Depression Association of America. (n.d.). *Generalized anxiety disorder.* Retrieved from https://adaa.org/sites/default/files/ADAA_GeneralAnxietyDisorderBrochure.pdf.

Anxiety and Depression Association of America. (n.d.). *Posttraumatic stress disorder.* Retrieved from https://adaa.org/sites/default/files/ADAA_PTSD.pdf.

Anxiety and Depression Association of America. (n.d.). *Social anxiety disorder.* Retrieved from https://adaa.org/sites/default/files/SocialAnxietyDisorderbrochure.pdf.

Anxiety and Depression Association of America. (n.d.). *Treating anxiety disorders.* Retrieved from https://adaa.org/sites/default/files/Treating%20Anxiety%20Disorders.pdf.

Ashcraft, M., & Kirk, E. (2001). The relationships among working memory, math anxiety, and performance. *Journal of Experimental Psychology: General, 130*(2), 224–237.

Bandelow, B., Michaelis, S., & Wedekind, D. (2017). Treatment of anxiety disorders. *Dialogues in Clinical Neuroscience, 19*(2), 93–107.

Beuke, C., Fischer, R., & McDowall, J. (2003). Anxiety and depression: Why and how to measure their separate effects. *Clinical Psychology Review, 23*(6), 831–848.

Borelli, J., Sbarra, D., Crowley, M., & Mayes, L. (2011). Mood symptoms and emotional responsiveness to threat in school-aged children. *Journal of Clinical Child & Adolescent Psychology, 40*(2), 220–232.

Bradley, R., & Corwyn, R. (2002). Socioeconomic status and child development. *Annual Review of Psychology, 53*, 371–399.

Chansky, T. (2014). *Freeing your child from anxiety.* New York, Random House LLC.

Cherry, K. (2019, November 27). *What is resilience?* Retrieved from https://www.verywellmind.com/what-is-resilience-2795059.

Child Mind Institute. (2018). *Anxiety and depression in adolescence.* Retrieved from https://childmind.org/report/2017-childrens-mental-health-report/anxiety-depression-adolescence/#_ftnref2.

Child Mind Institute. (n.d.). *A teacher's guide to OCD in the classroom.* Retrieved from https://childmind.org/guide/a-teachers-guide-to-ocd-in-the-classroom/.

Child Mind Institute. (2017). *2016 Children's mental health report.* Retrieved from https://childmind.org/report/2016-childrens-mental-health-report/.

Columbia University Medical Center. (2018, January 31). *'Anxiety cells' identified in the brain's hippocampus.* Retrieved from https://www.sciencedaily.com/releases/2018/01/180131133345.htm.

Conway, K., Swendsen, J., Husky, M., He, J., & Merikangas, K. (2016). Association of lifetime mental disorders and subsequent alcohol and illicit drug use: Results from the National Comorbidity Survey-Adolescent Supplement. *American Academy of Child and Adolescent Psychiatry, 55*(4), 280–288.

Data Resources Center for Child & Adolescent Health. (2017). *2016-2017 National survey of children's health.* Retrieved from https://www.childhealthdata.org/browse/survey/results?q=5415&r=1.

de Visser, L., van der Knaap, L., van de Loo, A., van der Weerd, C., Ohl, F., & van den Bos, R. (2010). Trait anxiety affects decision-making differently in healthy men and women: Towards gender-specific endophenotypes of anxiety. *Neuropsychologia, 48*(6), 1598–1606.

Dobson, C. (2012). *Effects of academic anxiety on the performance of students with and without learning disabilities and how students can cope with anxiety at school.* (Unpublished master's thesis). Northern Michigan University, Marquette, Michigan.

Economic and Social Research Council. (2009, June 26). *Anxiety's hidden cost in academic performance.* Retrieved from https://www.sciencedaily.com/releases/2009/06/090623090713.htm.

Edwards, D., & Cadenhead, C. (2009, May 1). *Understanding mental disorders in youth.* Retrieved from https://www.schoolcounselor.org/magazine/blogs/may-june-2009/understanding-mental-disorders-in-youth.

Ehmke, R. (n.d.). *Anxiety in the classroom.* Retrieved from https://childmind.org/article/classroom-anxiety-in-children/.

Eysenck, M., Derakshan, N., Santos, R., & Calvo, M. (2007). Anxiety and cognitive performance: Attentional control theory. *Emotion, 7*(2), 336–353.

Feldman, A. (2018a, November 2). *Treatments for anxiety.* Retrieved from https://www.medicalnewstoday.com/articles/323494.

Faubion, D. (2020, March 20). *Best Affirmations for anxiety.* Retrieved from https://www.betterhelp.com/advice/anxiety/best-affirmations-for-anxiety/.

Feldman, A. (2018b, October 26). *What causes anxiety?* Retrieved from https://www.medicalnewstoday.com/articles/323456.

Fowler, P., Tompsett, C., Braciszewski, J., Jacques-Tiura, A., & Balte, B. (2009). Community violence: A meta-analysis on the effect of exposure and mental health outcomes of children and adolescents. *Developmental Psychopathology, 21*(1), 227–259.

Ginsburg, G., Becker-Haimes, E., Keeton, C., Kendall, P., Iyengar, S., Sakolsky, D., & Piacentini, J. (2018). Results from the child/adolescent anxiety multimodal extended long-term study (CAMELS): Primary anxiety outcomes. *Journal of the American Academy of Child & Adolescent Psychiatry, 57*(7), 471–480.

Ginsburg, K., & Kinsman, S. (2014, September/October). Students with anxiety: Help struggling teens. *ASCA School Counselor, 51*(1), 14–17.

Glasofer, D. (2019a, August 20). *An overview of generalized anxiety disorder.* Retrieved from https://www.verywellmind.com/generalized-anxiety-disorder-4157247.

Glasofer, D. (2019b, November 17). *The physical symptoms of anxiety.* Retrieved from https://www.verywellmind.com/physical-symptoms-of-anxiety-1393151.

Goldstein, C. (n.d.). *What to do (and not do) when children are anxious.* Retrieved from https://childmind.org/article/what-to-do-and-not-do-when-children-are-anxious/.

Good Therapy. (n.d.). *Isolation.* Retrieved from https://www.goodtherapy.org/learn-about-therapy/issues/isolation.

Gotter, A. (2018, April 20). *What is the 4-7-8 breathing technique?* Retrieved from https://www.healthline.com/health/4-7-8-breathing#1.

Gregoire, C. (2013, May 23). *Meditation For Kids: Parents Turn to Mindfulness Practices to Help Children Stay Calm.* Retrieved from https://www.huffpost.com/entry/meditation-for-kids_n_3318721.

Guindon, M. (2002). Toward accountability in the use of the self-esteem construct. *Journal of Counseling and Development, 80*(2), 204–214.

Henry, A. (2019, July 9). *What anxiety does to your brain and what you can do about it.* Retrieved from https://lifehacker.com/what-anxiety-actually-does-to-you-and-what-you-can-do-a-1468128356.

Hudley, C., Daoud, A., Polanco, T., Wright-Castro, R., & Hershberg, R. (2003, April). *Student engagement, school climate and future expectations in high school.* Paper presented at the 2003 Biennial Meeting of the Society for Research in Child Development, Tampa, FL.

Hurley, K. (n.d.). *Classroom accommodations to help the anxious child at school.* Retrieved from http://psycdoc.com/net/classroom-help-anxious-child-at-school.

International OCD Foundation. (n.d.) *Impact of anxiety/OCD at school.* Retrieved from https://anxietyintheclassroom.org/school-system/i-want-to-learn-more/anxiety-impact-school/.

Kataoka, S., Zhang, L., & Wells, K. (2002). Unmet need for mental health care among US children: Variation by ethnicity and insurance status. *American Journal of Psychiatry, 159*(9), 1548–1555.

Kelly, O. (2019, November 25). *Anxiety disorder symptoms, diagnosis, and treatments.* Retrieved from https://www.verywellmind.com/anxiety-disorder-2510539.

Kennard, J. (2018, July 24). *20 Classroom interventions for children with anxiety disorders.* Retrieved from https://www.healthcentral.com/article/20-classroom-interventions-for-children-with-anxiety-disorders.

Leventhal, T., & Brooks-Gunn, J. (2000). The neighborhoods they live in: The effects of neighborhood residence on child and adolescent outcomes. *Psychological Bulletin, 126*(2), 309–337.

Low, K. (2019, October 1). *Understanding generalized anxiety disorder in children.* Retrieved from https://www.verywellmind.com/gad-in-children-20759.

Mayo Clinic. (n.d.) *Generalized anxiety disorder.* Retrieved from https://www.mayoclinic.org/diseases-conditions/generalized-anxiety-disorder/care-at-mayo-clinic/generalized-anxiety-disorder-care-at-mayo-clinic/ovc-20361172.

McCormac, M. (2016, September/October). Address student anxiety. *ASCA School Counselor, 53*(1), 12–17.

McKibben, S. (2017). Helping ease student anxiety. *ASCD Education Update, 59*(8), 4–5.

MentalHelp.net. (2020, March 29). *Types of stressors: Eustress vs distress.* Retrieved from https://www.mentalhelp.net/stress/types-of-stressors-eustress-vs-distress/.

Merikangas, K., Hep, J., Burstein, M., Swanson, S., Avenevoli, S., Cui, L., & Swendsen, J. (2010). Lifetime prevalence of mental disorders in U.S. adolescents: Results from the National Comorbidity Survey Replication--Adolescent Supplement (NCS-A). *Journal of American Academy of Child and Adolescent Psychiatry, 49*(10), 980–989.

Merikangas, K., Hep, J., Burstein, M., Swendsen, J., Avenevoli, S., Case, B., & Olfson, M. (2011). Service utilization for lifetime mental disorders in U.S. adolescents: Results of the national comorbidity survey adolescent supplement (NCS-A). *Journal of the American Academy of Child and Adolescent Psychiatry, 50*(1), 32–45.

Merriam-Webster. (n.d.). Anxiety. In *Merriam-Webster.com dictionary.* Retrieved from https://www.merriam-webster.com/dictionary/anxiety.

Morin, A. (n.d.) *Classroom accommodations for anxiety.* Understood. Retrieved from https://www.understood.org/en/learning-thinking-differences/treatments-approaches/educational-strategies/common-classroom-accommodations-and-modifications.

Mousavi, S., Low, W., & Hashim, A. (2016). Perceived parenting styles and cultural influences in adolescent's anxiety: A cross-cultural comparison. *Journal of Child & Family Studies, 25*(7), 2102–2110.

National Alliance of Mental Illness. (2017, December). *Anxiety disorders.* Retrieved from https://www.nami.org/About-Mental-Illness/Mental-Health-Conditions/Anxiety-Disorders.

National Center for Education Statistics. (2006, June). *The condition of education.* Retrieved from https://nces.ed.gov/pubs2006/2006071.pdf.

National Scientific Council on the Developing Child. (2010, February). *Persistent fear and anxiety can affect young children's learning and development.* Retrieved from https://developingchild.harvard.edu/wp-content/uploads/2010/05/Persistent-Fear-and-Anxiety-Can-Affect-Young-Childrens-Learning-and-Development.pdf.

Nelson, K. (2019, October 1). *10 Ways to help students who struggle with anxiety.* Retrieved from https://www.weareteachers.com/7-ways-to-help-students-who-struggle-with-anxiety/.

Nesse, R. (2006). Darwinian medicine and mental disorders. *International Congress Series, 1296,* 83–94.

No Panic. (n.d.). *Positive affirmations.* Retrieved from https://nopanic.org.uk/positive-affirmations/.

Owens, M., Norgate, R., & Hadwin, J. (2012). Anxiety and depression in academic performance: An exploration of the mediating factors of worry and working memory. *School Psychology International, 33*(4), 433–449.

Pergamin-Hight, L., Naim, R., Bakermans-Kranenburg, M., van IJzendoorn, M., & Bar-Haim, Y. (2015) Content specificity of attention bias to threat in anxiety disorders: A meta-analysis. *Clinical Psychology Review, 35,* 10–18.

Psychology Today. (n.d.). *Fear.* Retrieved from https://www.psychologytoday.com/us/basics/fear.

Raffety, B., Smith, R., & Ptacek, J. (1997). Facilitating and debilitating trait anxiety, situational anxiety, and coping with an anticipated stressor: A process analysis. *Journal of Personality and Social Psychology, 72*(4), 892–906.

Rauch, J. (2017, May 23). *Different types of anxiety disorders: How are they classified?* Retrieved from https://www.talkspace.com/blog/different-types-anxiety-disorders-classified/.

Remes, O., Brayne, C., van der Linde, R., & Lafortune, L. (2016). A systematic review of reviews on the prevalence of anxiety disorders in adult populations. *Brain and Behavior, 6*(7), 1–33.

Salcedo, B. (2018, January 19). *The comorbidity of anxiety and depression.* Retrieved from https://www.nami.org/Blogs/NAMI-Blog/January-2018/The-Comorbidity-of-Anxiety-and-Depression.

Santiago, C., Kaltman, S., & Miranda, J. (2013). Poverty and mental health: How do low-income adults and children fare in psychotherapy? *Journal of Clinical Psychology, 69*(2), 115–126.

Scott, E. (2019, June 24). *Reduce stress and improve your life with positive self talk.* Retrieved from https://www.verywellmind.com/how-to-use-positive-self-talk-for-stress-relief-3144816.

Scott, E. (2020, February 13). *When stress is actually good for you.* Retrieved from https://www.verywellmind.com/what-kind-of-stress-is-good-for-you-3145055.

Smith, M., Robinson, L., & Segal, J. (2019, October). *Anxiety disorders and anxiety attacks.* Retrieved from https://www.helpguide.org/articles/anxiety/anxiety-disorders-and-anxiety-attacks.htm.

The American Institute of Stress. (2019, October 21). *The good stress: How eustress makes you grow.* Retrieved from https://www.stress.org/the-good-stress-how-eustress-helps-you-grow.

The Brain from Top to Bottom. (n.d.). *Brain abnormalities associated with anxiety disorders.* Retrieved from https://thebrain.mcgill.ca/flash/d/d_08/d_08_cr/d_08_cr_anx/d_08_cr_anx.html.

Toyota Industries Corporation. (n.d.). *The Story of Sakichi Toyoda.* Retrieved from https://www.toyota-industries.com/company/history/toyoda_sakichi/.

Truluck, B. (2019, January/February). Stress busters. *ASCA School Counselor, 56*(3), 34–38.

Twenge, J.M., (2015). Time period and birth cohort differences in depressive symptoms in the U.S., 1982–2013. *Social Indicators Research, 121*(2), 437–454.

Tye, K. (2015, June 22). *How Anxiety Destroys Relationships (and How to Stop It).* Retrieved from https://www.goodtherapy.org/blog/how-anxiety-destroys-relationships-and-how-to-stop-it-0622155.

US Department of Health and Human Services (2000). *Mental health: A report of the surgeon general.* Rockville, MD.

Wadsworth., M., & Achenbach, T. (2005). Explaining the link between low socioeconomic status and psychopathology: Testing two mechanisms of the social causation hypothesis. *Journal of Consulting and Clinical Psychology, 73*(6), 1146–1153.

Washington, T., Rose, T., Coard, S., Patton, D., Young, S., Giles, S., & Nolen, M. (2017). Family-level factors, depression, and anxiety among African American children: A systematic review. *Child & Youth Care Forum, 46*(1), 137–156.

Waters, S., West, T., & Berry Mendes, W. (2014). Stress contagion: Physiological covariation between mothers and infants. *Association for Psychological Science, 25*(4), 934–942.

Way Ahead Mental Health Association. (2016, March 17). *Small steps: Strategies to support anxious children.* Retrieved from http://understandinganxiety.wayahead.org.au/download/strategies-to-support-anxious-children-in-the-classroom/.

Index

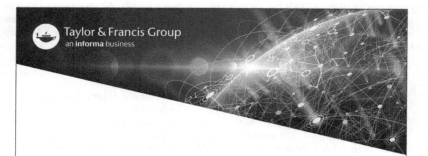